BY EVELYN WAUGH

Novels
DECLINE AND FALL
VILE BODIES
BLACK MISCHIEF
A HANDFUL OF DUST
SCOOP
PUT OUT MORE FLAGS
WORK SUSPENDED
BRIDESHEAD REVISITED
SCOTT-KING'S MODERN EUROPE
THE LOVED ONE
HELENA
MEN AT ARMS
LOVE AMONG THE RUINS
OFFICERS AND GENTLEMEN
UNCONDITIONAL SURRENDER
THE ORDEAL OF GILBERT PINFOLD

Biography
ROSSETTI
EDMUND CAMPION
MSGR. RONALD KNOX

Autobiography
A LITTLE LEARNING

Travel
LABELS
REMOTE PEOPLE
NINETY-TWO DAYS
WAUGH IN ABYSSINIA
ROBBERY UNDER LAW
WHEN THE GOING WAS GOOD
A TOURIST IN AFRICA

Short Stories
MR. LOVEDAY'S LITTLE OUTING, AND OTHER SAD STORIES
BASIL SEAL RIDES AGAIN

The Ordeal of Gilbert Pinfold

The Ordeal of Gilbert Pinfold

A CONVERSATION PIECE

by EVELYN WAUGH

Little, Brown and Company
BOSTON · TORONTO

LIBRARY OF CONGRESS CATALOG CARD NO. 57-9369

REPUBLISHED MARCH 1979

PRINTED IN THE UNITED STATES OF AMERICA

To
Daphne
in the belief that
her abounding sympathy
will extend even to poor
Pinfold

Note

THREE YEARS AGO Mr. Waugh suffered a brief
bout of hallucination closely resembling what is
here described. It was an interesting experience for a
man whose business is story-telling. Hallucination is
far removed from loss of reason. The reason works
with enhanced power, while the materials for it to
work on, presented by the senses, are delusions. A
story-teller naturally tries to find a plot into which his
observations can be fitted.

Much that was tediously repetitive has been omitted. Nothing of importance has been added. Mr.
Waugh does not deny that "Mr. Pinfold" is largely
based on himself. Subsidiary characters are fictitious.

Since his disconcerting voyage he has learned that
a great number of sane people suffer in this way from
time to time. He believes this record may amuse
them.

Contents

The Ordeal of Gilbert Pinfold

◄【 1 】►

Portrait
of the
Artist
in Middle Age

IT MAY HAPPEN in the next hundred years that the English novelists of the present day will come to be valued as we now value the artists and craftsmen of the late eighteenth century. The originators, the exuberant men, are extinct and in their place subsists and modestly flourishes a generation notable for elegance and variety of contrivance. It may well happen that there are lean years ahead in which our posterity will look back hungrily to this period, when there was so much will and so much ability to please.

Among these novelists Mr. Gilbert Pinfold stood quite high. At the time of his adventure, at the age of fifty, he had written a dozen books all of which

3

were still bought and read. They were translated into most languages and in the United States of America enjoyed intermittent but lucrative seasons of favour. Foreign students often chose them as the subject for theses, but those who sought to detect cosmic significance in Mr. Pinfold's work, to relate it to fashions in philosophy, social predicaments or psychological tensions, were baffled by his frank, curt replies to their questionnaires; their fellows in the English Literature School who chose more egotistical writers often found their theses more than half composed for them. Mr. Pinfold gave nothing away. Not that he was secretive or grudging by nature; he had nothing to give these students. He regarded his books as objects which he had made, things quite external to himself to be used and judged by others. He thought them well made, better than many reputed works of genius, but he was not vain of his accomplishment, still less of his reputation. He had no wish to obliterate anything he had written, but he would dearly have liked to revise it, envying painters, who are allowed to return to the same theme time and time again, clarifying and enriching until they have done all they can with it. A novelist is condemned to produce a succession of novelties,

4

new names for characters, new incidents for his plots, new scenery; but, Mr. Pinfold maintained, most men harbour the germs of one or two books only; all else is professional trickery of which the most daemonic of the masters — Dickens and Balzac even — were flagrantly guilty.

At the beginning of this fifty-first year of his life Mr. Pinfold presented to the world most of the attributes of well-being. Affectionate, high-spirited and busy in childhood; dissipated and often despairing in youth; sturdy and prosperous in early manhood; he had in middle age degenerated less than many of his contemporaries. He attributed this superiority to his long, lonely, tranquil days at Lychpole, a secluded village some hundred miles from London.

He was devoted to a wife many years younger than himself, who actively farmed the small property. Their children were numerous, healthy, good-looking and good-mannered, and his income just sufficed for their education. Once he had travelled widely; now he spent most of the year in the shabby old house which, over the years, he had filled with pictures and books and furniture of the kind he relished. As a soldier he had sustained in good heart

5

much discomfort and some danger. Since the end of the war his life had been strictly private. In his own village he took very lightly the duties which he might have thought incumbent on him. He contributed adequate sums to local causes but he had no interest in sport or in local government, no ambition to lead or to command. He had never voted in a parliamentary election, maintaining an idiosyncratic toryism which was quite unrepresented in the political parties of his time, and was regarded by his neighbours as being almost as sinister as socialism.

These neighbours were typical of the English countryside of the period. A few rich men farmed commercially on a large scale; a few had business elsewhere and came home merely to hunt; the majority were elderly and in reduced circumstances; people who, when the Pinfolds settled at Lychpole, lived comfortably with servants and horses, and now lived in much smaller houses and met at the fishmonger's. Many of these were related to one another and formed a compact little clan. Colonel and Mrs. Bagnold, Mr. and Mrs. Graves, Mrs. and Miss Fawdle, Colonel and Miss Garbett, Lady Fawdle-Upton and Miss Clarissa Bagnold all lived in a radius of ten miles from Lychpole. All were in some way related. In the first years of their marriage Mr. and Mrs. Pinfold had dined in all these households and had them to dine in return. But after the war the decline of fortune, less sharp in the Pinfolds' case than their neighbours', made their meetings less frequent. The Pinfolds were addicted to nicknames and each of these surrounding families had its own private, unsuspected appellation at Lychpole, not malicious but mildly derisive, taking its origin in most cases from some half-forgotten incident in the past. The nearest neighbour, whom they saw most often, was Reginald Graves-Upton, an uncle of the Graves-Uptons ten miles distant at Upper Mewling; a gentle, bee-keeping old bachelor who inhabited a thatched cottage up the lane less than a mile from the Manor. It was his habit on Sunday mornings to walk to church across the Pinfolds' fields and leave his Cairn terrier in the Pinfolds' stables while he attended Matins. He called for a quarter of an hour when he came to fetch his dog, drank a small glass of sherry and described the wireless programmes he had heard during the preceding week. This refined, fastidious old gentleman went by the recondite name of "the Bruiser," some-

7

times varied to "Pug," "Basher" and "Old Fisticuffs," all of which sobriquets derived from "Boxer"; for in recent years he had added to his few interests an object which he reverently referred to as "The Box."

This Box was one of many operating in various parts of the country. It was installed under the sceptical noses of Reginald Graves-Upton's nephew and niece at Upper Mewling. Mrs. Pinfold, who had been taken to see it, said it looked like a makeshift wireless set. According to the Bruiser and other devotees The Box exercised diagnostic and therapeutic powers. Some part of a sick man or animal — a hair, a drop of blood preferably — was brought to The Box, whose guardian would then "tune in" to the "Life-Waves" of the patient, discern the origin of the malady and prescribe treatment.

Mr. Pinfold was as sceptical as the younger Graves-Uptons. Mrs. Pinfold thought there must be something in it, because it had been tried, without her knowledge, on Lady Fawdle-Upton's nettle-rash and immediate relief had followed.

"It's all suggestion," said young Mrs. Graves-Upton.

"It can't be suggestion, if she didn't know it was being done," said Mr. Pinfold.

8

"No. It's simply a matter of measuring the Life-Waves," said Mrs. Pinfold.

"An extremely dangerous device in the wrong hands," said Mr. Pinfold.

"No, no. That is the beauty of it. It can't do any harm. You see it only transmits *Life* Forces. Fanny Graves tried it on her spaniel for worms, but they simply grew enormous with all the Life Force going into them. Like serpents, Fanny said."

"I should have thought this Box counted as sorcery," Mr. Pinfold said to his wife when they were alone. "You ought to confess it."

"D'you really think so?"

"No, not really. It's just a lot of harmless nonsense."

The Pinfolds' religion made a slight but perceptible barrier between them and these neighbours, a large part of whose activities centred round their parish churches. The Pinfolds were Roman Catholic, Mrs. Pinfold by upbringing, Mr. Pinfold by a later development. He had been received into the Church — "conversion" suggests an event more sudden and emotional than his calm acceptance of the propositions of his faith — in early manhood, at the time

9

when many Englishmen of humane education were falling into communism. Unlike them Mr. Pinfold remained steadfast. But he was reputed bigoted rather than pious. His trade by its nature is liable to the condemnation of the clergy as, at the best, frivolous; at the worst, corrupting. Moreover by the narrow standards of the age his habits of life were self-indulgent and his utterances lacked prudence. And at the very time when the leaders of his Church were exhorting their people to emerge from the catacombs into the forum, to make their influence felt in democratic politics and to regard worship as a corporate rather than a private act, Mr. Pinfold burrowed ever deeper into the rock. Away from his parish he sought the least frequented Mass; at home he held aloof from the multifarious organizations which have sprung into being at the summons of the hierarchy to redeem the times. He was sometimes referred to as a leading Catholic but his leadership was not conspicuous.

But Mr. Pinfold was far from friendless and he set great store by his friends. They were the men and women who were growing old with him, whom in the 1920s and '30s he had seen constantly; who in the diaspora of the '40s and '50s kept more tenuous touch with one another, the men at Bellamy's Club, the women at the half-dozen poky, pretty houses of Westminster and Belgravia to which had descended the larger hospitality of a happier age.

He had made no new friends in late years. Sometimes he thought he detected a slight coldness among his old cronies. It was always he, it seemed to him, who proposed a meeting. It was always they who first rose to leave. In particular there was one, Roger Stillingfleet, who had once been an intimate but now seemed to avoid him. Roger Stillingfleet was a writer, one of the few Mr. Pinfold really liked. He knew of no reason for their estrangement and, enquiring, was told that Roger had grown very odd lately. He never came in Bellamy's now, it was said, except to collect his letters or to entertain a visiting American.

It sometimes occurred to Mr. Pinfold that he must be growing into a bore. His opinions certainly were easily predictable.

His strongest tastes were negative. He abhorred plastics, Picasso, sunbathing and jazz — everything in fact that had happened in his own lifetime. The tiny kindling of charity which came to him through his religion sufficed only to temper his disgust and

11

change it to boredom. There was a phrase in the 'thirties: "It is later than you think," which was designed to cause uneasiness. It was never later than Mr. Pinfold thought. At intervals during the day and night he would look at his watch and learn always with disappointment how little of his life was past, how much there was still ahead of him. He wished no one ill, but he looked at the world *sub specie aeternitatis* and he found it flat as a map; except when, rather often, personal annoyance intruded. Then he would come tumbling from his exalted point of observation. Shocked by a bad bottle of wine, an impertinent stranger, or a fault in syntax, his mind like a cinema camera trucked furiously forward to confront the offending object close up with glaring lens; with the eyes of a drill sergeant inspecting an awkward squad, bulging with wrath that was half facetious, and with half-simulated incredulity; like a drill sergeant he was absurd to many but to some rather formidable.

Once upon a time all this had been thought diverting. People quoted his pungent judgments and invented anecdotes of his audacity, which were recounted as "typical Pinfolds." Now, he realized, his singularity had lost some of its attraction for others, but he was too old a dog to learn new tricks.

As a boy, at the age of puberty when most of his school fellows coarsened, he had been as fastidious as the Bruiser and in his early years of success diffidence had lent him charm. Prolonged prosperity had wrought the change. He had seen sensitive men make themselves a protective disguise against the rebuffs and injustices of manhood. Mr. Pinfold had suffered little in these ways; he had been tenderly reared and, as a writer, welcomed and over-rewarded early. It was his modesty which needed protection and for this purpose, but without design, he gradually assumed this character of burlesque. He was neither a scholar nor a regular soldier; the part for which he cast himself was a combination of eccentric don and testy colonel and he acted it strenuously, before his children at Lychpole and his cronies in London, until it came to dominate his whole outward personality. When he ceased to be alone, when he swung into his club or stumped up the nursery stairs, he left half of himself behind and the other half swelled to fill its place. He offered the world a front of pomposity mitigated by indiscretion that was as hard, bright and antiquated as a cuirass.

Mr. Pinfold's nanny used to say: "Don't care went

13

to the gallows"; also "Sticks and stones can break my bones, but words can never hurt me." Mr. Pinfold did not care what the village or his neighbours said of him. As a little boy he had been acutely sensitive to ridicule. His adult shell seemed impervious. He had long held himself inaccessible to interviewers and the young men and women who were employed to write "profiles" collected material where they could. Every week his press-cutting agents brought to his breakfast-table two or three rather offensive allusions. He accepted without much resentment the world's estimate of himself. It was part of the price he paid for privacy. There were also letters from strangers, some abusive, some adulatory. Mr. Pinfold was unable to discover any particular superiority of taste or expression in the writers of either sort. To both he sent printed acknowledgments.

His days passed in writing, reading and managing his own small affairs. He had never employed a secretary and for the last two years he had been without a manservant. But Mr. Pinfold did not repine. He was perfectly competent to answer his own letters, pay his bills, tie his parcels and fold his clothes. At night his most frequent recurring dream was of doing the *Times* cross-word puzzle; his most disagreeable that he was reading a tedious book aloud to his family.

Physically, in his late forties, he had become lazy. Time was, he rode to hounds, went for long walks, dug his garden, felled small trees. Now he spent most of the day in an arm-chair. He ate less, drank more, and grew corpulent. He was very seldom so ill as to spend a day in bed. He suffered intermittently from various twinges and brief bouts of pain in his joints and muscles — arthritis, gout, rheumatism, fibrositis; they were not dignified by any scientific name. Mr. Pinfold seldom consulted his doctor. When he did so it was as a "private patient." His children availed themselves of the National Health Act but Mr. Pinfold was reluctant to disturb a relationship which had been formed in his first years at Lychpole. Dr. Drake, Mr. Pinfold's medical attendant, had inherited the practice from his father and had been here before the Pinfolds came to Lychpole. Lean, horsy and weatherbeaten in appearance, he had deep roots and wide ramifications in the countryside, being brother of the local auctioneer, brother-in-law of the solicitor, and cousin of three neighbouring rectors. His recreations were sporting.

15

He was not a man of high technical pretensions but he suited Mr. Pinfold well. He too suffered, more sharply, from Mr. Pinfold's troubles and when consulted remarked that Mr. Pinfold must expect these things at his age, that the whole district was troubled in this way and that Lychpole was notoriously the worst spot in it.

Mr. Pinfold also slept badly. It was a trouble of long standing. For twenty-five years he had used various sedatives, for the last ten years a single specific, chloral and bromide which, unknown to Dr. Drake, he bought on an old prescription in London. There were periods of literary composition when he would find the sentences he had written during the day running in his head, the words shifting and changing colour kaleidoscopically, so that he would again and again climb out of bed, pad down to the library, make a minute correction, return to his room, lie in the dark dazzled by the pattern of vocables until obliged once more to descend to the manuscript. But those days and nights of obsession, of what might without vainglory be called "creative" work, were a small part of his year. On most nights he was neither fretful nor apprehensive. He was merely bored. After even the idlest day he demanded six or seven hours of insensibility. With them behind him, with them to look forward to, he could face another idle day with something approaching jauntiness; and these his doses unfailingly provided.

At about the time of his fiftieth birthday there occurred two events which seemed trivial at the time but grew to importance in his later adventures. The first of these primarily concerned Mrs. Pinfold. During the war Lychpole was let, the house to a convent, the fields to a grazier. This man, Hill, had collected parcels of grass-land in and around the parish and on them kept a nondescript herd of "unattested" dairy-cattle. The pasture was rank, the fences dilapidated. When the Pinfolds came home in 1945 and wanted their fields back, the War Agricultural Committee, normally predisposed towards the sitting tenant, were in no doubt of their decision in Mrs. Pinfold's favour. Had she acted at once, Hill would have been out, with his compensation, at Michaelmas, but Mrs. Pinfold was tender-hearted and Hill was adroit. First he pleaded, then having established new rights, asserted them. Lady Day succeeded Michaelmas; Michaelmas, Lady Day for

17

four full years. Hill retreated meadow by meadow. The committee, still popularly known as "the War Ag.," returned, walked the property anew, again found for Mrs. Pinfold. Hill, who now had a lawyer, appealed. So it went on. Mr. Pinfold held aloof from it all, merely noting with sorrow the anxiety of his wife. At length at Michaelmas 1949 Hill finally moved. He boasted in the village inn of his cleverness, and left for the other side of the county with a comfortable profit.

The second event occurred soon after. Mr. Pinfold received an invitation from the B.B.C. to record an "interview." In the previous twenty years there had been many such proposals and he had always refused them. This time the fee was more liberal and the conditions softer. He would not have to go to the offices in London. Electricians would come to him with their apparatus. No script had to be submitted; no preparation of any kind was required; the whole thing would take an hour. In an idle moment Mr. Pinfold agreed and at once regretted it.

The day came towards the end of the summer holidays. Soon after breakfast there arrived a motor-car, and a van of the sort used in the army by the more important kinds of signaller, which immediately absorbed the attention of the younger children. Out of the car there came three youngish men, thin of hair, with horn-rimmed elliptical spectacles, cord trousers and tweed coats; exactly what Mr. Pinfold was expecting. Their leader was named Angel. He emphasised his privacy by means of a neat, thick beard. He and his colleagues, he explained, had slept in the district, where he had an aunt. They would have to leave before luncheon. They would get through their business in the morning. The signallers began rapidly uncoiling wires and setting up their microphone in the library, while Mr. Pinfold drew the attention of Angel and his party to the more noticeable of his collection of works of art. They did not commit themselves to an opinion, merely remarking that the last house they visited had a gouache by Rouault.

"I didn't know he ever painted in gouache," said Mr. Pinfold. "Anyway he's a dreadful painter."

"Ah!" said Angel. "That's very nice. Very nice indeed. We must try and work that into the broadcast."

When the electricians had made their arrangements Mr. Pinfold sat at his table with the three strangers, a microphone in their midst. They were attempting to emulate a series that had been cleverly done in Paris with various French celebrities, in which informal, spontaneous discussion had seduced the objects of inquiry into self-revelation.

They questioned Mr. Pinfold in turn about his tastes and habits. Angel led and it was at him that Mr. Pinfold looked. The commonplace face above the beard became slightly sinister, the accentless, but insidiously plebeian voice, menacing. The questions were civil enough in form but Mr. Pinfold thought he could detect an underlying malice. Angel seemed to believe that anyone sufficiently eminent to be interviewed by him must have something to hide, must be an impostor whom it was his business to trap and expose, and to direct his questions from some basic, previous knowledge of something discreditable. There was the hint of the underdog's snarl which Mr. Pinfold recognised from his press-cuttings.

He was well equipped to deal with insolence, real or imagined, and answered succinctly and shrewdly, disconcerting his adversaries, if adversaries they were, point by point. When it was over Mr. Pinfold

20

offered his visitors sherry. Tension relaxed. He asked politely who was their next subject.

"We're going on to Stratford," said Angel, "to interview Cedric Thorne."

"You evidently have not seen this morning's paper," said Mr. Pinfold.

"No, we left before it came."

"Cedric Thorne has escaped you. He hanged himself yesterday afternoon in his dressing-room."

"Good heavens, are you sure?"

"It's in the *Times*."

"May I see?"

Angel was shaken from his professional calm. Mr. Pinfold brought the paper and he read the paragraph with emotion.

"Yes, yes. That's him. I half expected this. He was a personal friend. I must get on to his wife. May I phone?"

Mr. Pinfold apologized for the levity with which he had broken the news and led Angel to the business-room. He refilled the sherry glasses and attempted to appear genial. Angel returned shortly to say: "I couldn't get through. I'll have to try again later."

Mr. Pinfold repeated his regrets.

"Yes, it is a terrible thing — not wholly unexpected though."

A macabre note had been added to the discords of the morning.

Then hands were shaken; the vehicles turned on the gravel and drove away.

When they were out of sight down the turn of the drive, one of the children who had been listening to the conversation in the van said: "You didn't like those people much, did you, Papa?"

He had definitely not liked them and they left an unpleasant memory which grew sharper in the weeks before the record was broadcast. He brooded. It seemed to him that an attempt had been made against his privacy and he was not sure how effectively he had defended it. He strained to remember his precise words and his memory supplied various distorted versions. Finally the evening came when the performance was made public. Mr. Pinfold had the cook's wireless carried into the drawing-room. He and Mrs. Pinfold listened together. His voice came to him strangely old and fruity, but what he said gave him no regret. "They tried to make an ass of me," he said. "I don't believe they succeeded."

Mr. Pinfold for the time forgot Angel.

Boredom alone and some stiffness in the joints disturbed that sunny autumn. Despite his age and dangerous trade Mr. Pinfold seemed to himself and to others unusually free of the fashionable agonies of *angst*.

-◄2►-

Collapse
of
Elderly Party

M R. PINFOLD's idleness has been remarked. He was half-way through a novel and had stopped work in early summer. The completed chapters had been typed, rewritten, retyped, and lay in a drawer of his desk. He was entirely satisfied with them. He knew in a general way what had to be done to finish the book and he believed he could at any moment set himself to do it. But he was not pressed for money. The sales of his earlier works had already earned him that year the modest sufficiency which the laws of his country allowed. Further effort could only bring him sharply diminishing rewards and he was disinclined to effort. It was as though the characters he had quickened had fallen into a light doze, and he left them benevolently to them-

24

selves. Hard things were in store for them. Let them sleep while they could. All his life he had worked intermittently. In youth his long periods of leisure had been devoted to amusement. Now he had abandoned that quest. That was the main difference between Mr. Pinfold at fifty and Mr. Pinfold at thirty.

Winter set in sharp at the end of October. The central-heating plant at Lychpole was ancient and voracious. It had not been used since the days of fuel shortage. With most of the children away at school Mr. and Mrs. Pinfold withdrew into two rooms, heaped the fires with such coal as they could procure and sheltered from draughts behind screens and sandbags. Mr. Pinfold's spirits sank, he began to talk of the West Indies and felt the need of longer periods of sleep.

The composition of his sleeping-draught, as originally prescribed, was largely of water. He suggested to his chemist that it would save trouble to have the essential ingredients in full strength and to dilute them himself. Their taste was bitter and after various experiments he found they were most palatable in *crème de menthe*. He was not scrupulous in measuring the dose. He splashed into the glass as

25

much as his mood suggested and if he took too little and woke in the small hours he would get out of bed and make unsteadily for the bottles and a second swig. Thus he passed many hours in welcome unconsciousness; but all was not well with him. Whether from too much strong medicine or from some other cause, he felt decidedly seedy by the middle of November. He found himself disagreeably flushed, particularly after drinking his normal not illiberal quantity of wine and brandy. Crimson blotches appeared on the backs of his hands.

He called in Dr. Drake, who said: "That sounds like an allergy."

"Allergic to what?"

"Ah, that's hard to say. Almost anything can cause an allergy nowadays. It might be something you're wearing or some plant growing near. The only cure really is a change."

"I might go abroad after Christmas."

"Yes, that's the best thing you could do. Anyway don't worry. No one ever died of an allergy. It's allied to hay-fever," he added learnedly, "and asthma."

Another thing which troubled him, and which he soon began to attribute to his medicine, was the behaviour of his memory. It began to play him tricks. He did not grow forgetful. He remembered everything in clear detail but he remembered it wrong. He would state a fact, dogmatically, sometimes in print — a date, a name, a quotation — find himself challenged, turn to his books for verification and find most disconcertingly that he was at fault.

Two incidents of this kind slightly alarmed him. With the idea of cheering him up Mrs. Pinfold invited a week-end party to Lychpole. On the Sunday afternoon he proposed a visit to a remarkable tomb in a neighbouring church. He had not been there since the war, but he had a clear image of it, which he described to them in technical detail; a recumbent figure of the mid-sixteenth century in gilded bronze; something almost unique in England. They found the place without difficulty; it was unquestionably what they sought; but the figure was of coloured alabaster. They laughed, he laughed, but he was shocked.

The second incident was more humiliating. A friend in London, James Lance, who shared his tastes in furniture, found, and offered him as a present, a most remarkable piece; a wash-hand stand

27

of the greatest elaboration designed by an English architect of the 1860s, a man not universally honoured but of magisterial status to Mr. Pinfold and his friends.

This massive freak of fancy was decorated with metal work and mosaic, and with a series of panels painted in his hot youth by a rather preposterous artist who later became President of the Royal Academy. It was just such a trophy as Mr. Pinfold most valued. He hurried to London, studied the object with exultation, arranged for its delivery and impatiently awaited its arrival at Lychpole. A fortnight later it came, was borne upstairs and set in the space cleared for it. Then to his horror Mr. Pinfold observed that an essential part was missing. There should have been a prominent, highly ornamental, copper tap in the centre, forming the climax of the design. In its place there was merely a small socket. Mr. Pinfold broke into lamentation. The carriers asserted that this was the condition of the piece when they fetched it. Mr. Pinfold bade them search their van. Nothing was found. Mr. Pinfold surcharged the receipt "incomplete" and immediately wrote to the firm ordering a diligent search of the warehouse where the wash-

28

hand stand had reposed *en route* and enclosing a detailed drawing of the lost member. There was a brisk exchange of letters, the carriers denying all responsibility. Finally Mr. Pinfold, decently reluctant to involve the donor in a dispute about a gift, wrote to James Lance asking for corroboration. James Lance replied: there never had been any tap such as Mr. Pinfold described.

"You haven't always been altogether making sense lately," said Mrs. Pinfold when her husband showed her this letter, "and you're a very odd colour. Either you're drinking too much or doping too much, or both."

"I wonder if you're right," said Mr. Pinfold. "Perhaps I ought to go slow after Christmas."

The children's holidays were a time when Mr. Pinfold felt a special need for unconsciousness at night and for stimulated geniality by day. Christmas was always the worst season. During that dread week he made copious use of wine and narcotics and his inflamed face shone like the florid squireens depicted in the cards that littered the house. Once catching sight of himself in the looking glass, thus empurpled and wearing a paper crown, he took fright at what he saw.

"I *must* get away," said Mr. Pinfold later to his wife. "I must go somewhere sunny and finish my book."

"I wish I could come too. There's so much to be done getting Hill's horrible fields back into shape. I'm rather worried about you, you know. You ought to have someone to look after you."

"I'll be all right. I work better alone."

The cold grew intense. Mr. Pinfold spent the day crouched over the library fire. To leave it for the icy passages made him shudder and stumble, half benumbed, while outside the hidden sun glared over a landscape that seemed all turned to metal; lead and iron and steel. In the evenings only Mr. Pinfold managed a semblance of jollity, joining his family in charades or Up Jenkins, playing the fool to the loud delight of the youngest and the tolerant amuse-ment of the eldest of his children, until in degrees of age they went happily to their rooms and he was released into his own darkness and silence.

At length the holidays came to an end. Nuns and monks received their returning charges and Lych-pole was left in peace save for rare intrusions from the nursery. And now just when Mr. Pinfold was gathering himself as it were for a strenuous effort at reformation, he was struck down by the most severe attack of his "aches" which he had yet suffered. Every joint, but especially feet, ankles and knees, agonized him. Dr. Drake again advocated a warm climate and prescribed some pills which he said were "something new and pretty powerful." They were large and drab, reminding Mr. Pinfold of the pellets of blotting-paper which used to be rolled at his private school. Mr. Pinfold added them to his bromide and chloral and *crème de menthe*, his wine and gin and brandy, and to a new sleeping-draught which his doctor, ignorant of the existence of his other bottle, also supplied.

And now his mind became much overcast. One great thought excluded all others, the need to escape. He, who even in this extremity eschewed the telephone, telegraphed to the travel-agency with whom he dealt: "*Kindly arrange immediate passage West Indies, East Indies, Africa, India, anywhere hot, luxury preferred, private bath, outside single cabin essential,*" and anxiously awaited the reply. When it came it comprised a large envelope full of decorative folders and a note saying they awaited his further instructions.

Mr. Pinfold became frantic. He knew one of the

31

directors of the firm. He thought he had met others. It came to him in his daze quite erroneously that he had lately read somewhere that a lady of his acquaintance had joined the board. To all of them at their private addresses he despatched peremptory telegrams: *"Kindly investigate wanton inefficiency your office. Pinfold."*

The director whom he really knew took action. There was little choice at that moment. Mr. Pinfold was lucky to secure a passage on the *Caliban,* a one-class ship sailing in three days for Ceylon.

During the time of waiting Mr. Pinfold's frenzy subsided. He became instead intermittently comatose. When lucid he was in pain.

Mrs. Pinfold said, as she had often said before: "You're doped, darling, up to the eyes."

"Yes. It's those rheumatism pills. Drake said they were very strong."

Mr. Pinfold, who was normally rather deft, now became clumsy. He dropped things. He found his buttons and laces intractable, his handwriting in the few letters which his journey necessitated, uncertain, his spelling, never strong, wildly barbaric.

In one of his clearer hours he said to Mrs. Pinfold: "I believe you are right. I shall give up the sleeping-draughts as soon as I get to sea. I always sleep better at sea. I shall cut down on drink too. As soon as I get rid of these damned aches, I shall start work. I can always work at sea. I shall have the book finished before I get home."

These resolutions persisted; there was a sober, industrious time ahead of him in a few days' time. He had to survive somehow until then. Everything would come right very soon.

Mrs. Pinfold shared these hopes. She was busy with her plans for the farm, which the newly liberated territory made more elaborate. She could not get away. Nor did she think her presence was needed. Once her husband was safely on board, all would be well with him.

She helped him pack. Indeed he could do nothing except sit on a bedroom chair and give confused directions. He must take foolscap paper, he said, in large quantities; also ink, foreign ink was never satisfactory. And pens. He had once experienced great difficulty in New York in purchasing pen-nibs; he had in the end had recourse to a remote law-stationer's. All foreigners, he was now convinced, used some kind of stylographic instrument. He must take pens and nibs. His clothes were a matter of indif-

33

ference. You could always get a Chinaman, anywhere out of Europe, to make you a suit of clothes in an afternoon, Mr. Pinfold said.

That Sunday morning Mr. Pinfold did not go to Mass. He lay in bed until midday and, when he came down, hobbled to the drawing-room window and gazed across the bare, icy park thinking of the welcoming tropics. Then he said: "Oh, God, here comes the Bruiser."

"Hide."

"No fire in the library."

"I'll tell him you're ill."

"No. I like the Bruiser. Besides, if you say I'm ill, he'll get his damned Box to work on me."

Throughout the short visit Mr. Pinfold exerted himself to be affable.

"You aren't looking at all well, Gilbert," the Bruiser said.

"I'm all right really. A twinge of rheumatism. I'm sailing the day after tomorrow for Ceylon."

"That's very sudden, isn't it?"

"The weather. Need a change."

He sank into his chair and then, when the Bruiser left, got to his feet again with an enormous obvious effort.

"Please don't come out," said the Bruiser.

Mrs. Pinfold went with him to release his dog and when she returned found Mr. Pinfold enraged.

"I know what you two have been talking about."

"Do you? I was hearing about the Fawdles' row with the Parish Council about their right of way."

"You've been giving him my hair for his Box."

"Nonsense, Gilbert."

"I could tell by the way he looked at me that he was measuring my Life-Waves."

Mrs. Pinfold looked at him sadly. "You really are in rather a bad way, aren't you, darling?"

The *Caliban* was not a ship so large as to require a special train; carriages were reserved on the regular service from London. Mrs. Pinfold accompanied him there the day before his departure. He had to collect his tickets from the travel-agency, but when he arrived in London great lassitude came over him and he went straight to bed in his hotel, summoning a messenger from the agency to bring them to him. A young polite man came at once. He bore a small portfolio of documents, tickets for train and ship and for return by air, baggage forms, embarkation

35

cards, carbon copies of letters of reservation and the like. Mr. Pinfold had difficulty in understanding. He had trouble with his cheque book. The young man looked at him with more than normal curiosity. Perhaps he was a reader of Mr. Pinfold's works. It was more probable that he found something bizarre in the spectacle of Mr. Pinfold, lying there groaning and muttering, propped by pillows, purple in the face, with a bottle of champagne open beside him. Mr. Pinfold offered him a glass. He refused. When he had gone Mr. Pinfold said, "I didn't at all like the look of that young man."

"Oh, he was all right," said Mrs. Pinfold.

"There was something filthy about him," said Mr. Pinfold. "He stared at me as though he was measuring my Life-Waves."

Then he fell into a doze.

Mrs. Pinfold lunched alone downstairs and rejoined her husband, who said: "I must go and say good-bye to my mother. Order a car."

"Darling, you aren't well enough."

"I *always* say good-bye to her before going abroad. I've told her we are coming."

"I'll telephone and explain. Or shall I go out there alone?"

"I'm going. It's true I'm not well enough, but I'm going. Get the hall-porter to have a car here in half an hour."

Mr. Pinfold's widowed mother lived in a pretty little house at Kew. She was eighty-two years old, sharp of sight and hearing, but of recent years very slow of mind. In childhood Mr. Pinfold had loved her extravagantly. There remained now only a firm *pietas*. He no longer enjoyed her company nor wished to communicate. She had been left rather badly off by his father. Mr. Pinfold supplemented her income with payments under a deed of covenant so that she was now comfortably placed with a single, faithful old maid to look after her and all her favourite possessions, preserved from the larger house, set out around her.

Young Mrs. Pinfold, who would talk happily of her children, was very much more agreeable company to the old woman than was her son, but Mr. Pinfold went to call dutifully several times a year and, as he said, always before an absence of any length.

A funereal limousine bore them to Kew. Mr. Pinfold sat huddled in rugs. He hobbled on two sticks, one a blackthorn, the other a Malacca cane, through the little gate up the garden path. An hour later he was out again, subsiding with groans into the back of the car. The visit had not been a success.

"It wasn't a success, was it?" said Mr. Pinfold.

"We ought to have stayed to tea."

"She knows I never have tea."

"But I do, and Mrs. Yercombe had it all prepared. I saw it on a trolley — cakes and sandwiches and a muffin-dish."

"The truth is my mother doesn't like to see anyone younger than herself iller than herself — except children of course."

"You were beastly snubbing about the children."

"Yes. I know. Damn. Damn. Damn. I'll write to her from the ship. I'll send her a cable. Why does everyone except me find it so easy to be nice?"

When he reached the hotel he returned to bed and ordered another bottle of champagne. He dozed again. Mrs. Pinfold sat quietly reading a paper-covered detective story. He awoke and ordered a rather elaborate dinner, but by the time it came his appetite was gone. Mrs. Pinfold ate well, but sadly. When the table was wheeled out, Mr. Pinfold hobbled to the bath-room and took his blue-grey pills. Three a day was the number prescribed. He had a dozen left. He took a big dose of his sleeping-draught; the bottle was half full.

"I'm taking too much," he said, not for the first time. "I'll finish what I've got and never order any more." He looked at himself in the glass. He looked at the backs of his hands, which were again mottled with large crimson patches. "I'm sure it's not really good for me," he said and felt his way to bed, tumbled in and fell heavily asleep.

His train was at ten next day. The funereal limousine was ordered. Mr. Pinfold dressed laboriously and, without shaving, went to the station. Mrs. Pinfold came with him. He needed help to find a porter and to find his seat. He dropped his ticket and his sticks on the platform.

"I don't believe you ought to be going alone," said Mrs. Pinfold. "Wait for another ship and I'll come too."

"No, no. I shall be all right."

But some hours later when he reached the docks Mr. Pinfold did not feel so hopeful. He had slept most of the way, now and then waking to light a cigar and let it fall from his fingers after a few puffs. His aches seemed sharper than ever as he climbed out of the carriage. Snow was falling. The distance from the train to the ship seemed enormous. The other passengers stepped out briskly. Mr. Pinfold moved slowly. On the quay a telegraph boy was taking messages. Mrs. Pinfold would be back at Lychpole by now. Mr. Pinfold with great difficulty wrote: *"Safely embarked. All love."* Then he moved to the gangway and painfully climbed aboard.

A coloured steward led him to his cabin. He gazed round it unseeing, sitting on a bunk. There was something he ought to do: telegraph his mother. On the cabin table was some writing paper bearing the ship's name and the flag of the line at its head. Mr. Pinfold tried to compose and inscribe a message. The task proved to be one of insuperable difficulty. He threw the spoilt paper into the basket and sat on his bed, still in his hat and overcoat, with his sticks beside him. Presently his two suitcases arrived. He gazed at them for some time, then began to unpack. That too proved difficult. He rang his bell and the coloured steward re-appeared bowing and smiling.

"I'm not very well. I wonder if you could unpack for me?"

"Dinner seven-thirty o'clock, sir."

"I said, could you unpack for me?"

"No, sir, bar not open in port, sir."

The man smiled and bowed and left Mr. Pinfold.

Mr. Pinfold sat there, in his hat and coat, holding his cudgel and his cane. Presently an English steward appeared with the passenger list, some forms to fill, and the message: "The Captain's compliments, sir, and he would like to have the honour of your company at his table in the dining saloon."

"Now?"

"No, sir. Dinner is at seven-thirty. I don't expect the Captain will be dining in the saloon tonight."

"I don't think I shall either," said Mr. Pinfold. "Thank the Captain. Very civil of him. Another night. Someone said something about the bar not being open. Can't you get me some brandy?"

"Oh yes, sir. I think so, sir. Any particular brand?"

"Brandy," said Mr. Pinfold. "Large one."

The chief steward brought it with his own hands.

"Good-night," said Mr. Pinfold.

He found on the top of his case the things he needed for the night. Among them his pills and his bottle. The brandy impelled him to action. He must telegraph to his mother. He groped his way out and along the corridor to the purser's office. A clerk was on duty, very busy with his papers behind a grill.

"I want to send a telegram."

"Yes, sir. There's a boy at the head of the gang-way."

"I'm not feeling very well. I wonder if you could be very kind and write it for me?"

The purser looked at him hard, observed his un-shaven chin, smelled brandy, and drew on his long experience of travellers.

"Sorry about that, sir. Pleased to be any help."

Mr. Pinford dictated, *"Everyone in ship most help-ful. Love. Gilbert,"* fumbled with a handful of silver, then crept back to his cabin. There he took his large grey pills and a swig of his sleeping-draught. Then, prayerless, he got himself to bed.

◦◦ 3 ◦◦

An
Unhappy
Ship

THE SS *CALIBAN*, Captain Steerforth master, was middle-aged and middle class, clean, trustworthy and comfortable, without pretence to luxury. There were no private baths. Meals were not served in cabins, it was stated, except on the orders of the medical officer. Her public rooms were panelled in fumed oak in the fashion of an earlier generation. She plied between Liverpool and Rangoon, stopping at intermediate ports, carrying a mixed cargo and a more or less homogeneous company of passengers, Scotchmen and their wives mostly, travelling on business and on leave. Crew and stewards were Lascars.

When Mr. Pinfold came to himself it was full day

and he was rocking gently to and fro in his narrow bed with the slow roll of the high seas.

He had barely noticed his cabin on the preceding evening. Now he observed that it was a large one, with two berths. There was a little window made of slats of opaque glass, fitted with tight, ornamental muslin curtains, and a sliding shutter. This gave, not on the sea, but on a deck where people from time to time passed, casting a brief shadow but with no sound that was audible above the beat of the engine, the regular creak of plates and woodwork and the continuous insect-hum of the ventilator. The ceiling, at which Mr. Pinfold gazed, was spanned as though by a cottage beam by a white, studded air-shaft and by a multiplicity of pipes and electric cable. Mr. Pinfold lay for some time, gazing and rocking, not quite sure where he was but rather pleased than not to be there. His watch, unwound the night before, had run down. He had been called. On the shelf at his side a cup of tea, already quite cold, slopped in its saucer, and beside it, stained with spilt tea, was the ship's passenger list. He found himself entered as *Mr. G. Penfold* and thought of Mr. Pooter at the Mansion House. The misprint was welcome as an item of disguise, an uncovenanted addition to his privacy. He glanced idly through the other names — Dr. Abercrombie, Mr. Addison, Miss Amory, Mr. and Mrs. and Miss Margaret Angel, Mr. and Mrs. Benson, Mr. Blackadder, Major and Mrs. Cockson — no one he knew, no one likely to annoy him. There were half a dozen Burmese on their way to Rangoon; the rest were solidly British. No one, he felt confident, would have read his books or would seek to draw him into literary conversation. He would be able to do a quiet three weeks' work in this ship as soon as his health mended.

He sat up and put his feet to the floor. He was still crippled but a shade less painfully, he thought, than in the days before. He went to his basin. The looking-glass showed him a face which still looked alarmingly old and ill. He shaved, brushed his hair, took his grey pill, returned to bed with a book and at once fell into a doze.

The ship's hooter roused him. That must be twelve noon. A knock on his door, barely audible above the other sea noises, and the dark face of his steward appeared.

"No good today," the man said. "Plenty passenger sick."

He took the cup of tea and slipped away.

Mr. Pinfold was a good sailor. Only once, in a war which had been largely spent bucketing about in various sorts of boat, had he ever been sea-sick and on that occasion most of the naval crew had been prostrate also. Mr. Pinfold, who was neither beautiful nor athletic, cherished this one gift of parsimonious Nature. He decided to get up.

The main deck, when he reached it, was almost deserted. Two wind-blown girls in thick sweaters were tacking along arm-in-arm past the piles of folded chairs. Mr. Pinfold hobbled to the after smoking-room bar. Four or five men sat together in one corner. He nodded to them, found a chair on the further side and ordered brandy and ginger-ale.

He was not himself. He knew in a distant way, as he knew, or thought he knew, certain facts of history, that he was in a ship, travelling for the good of his health, but, as with much of his historical knowledge, he was vague about the date. He did not know that twenty-four hours ago he had been in the train from London to Liverpool. His phases of sleeping and waking in the last few days were not related to night and day. He sat still in the smoking-room gazing blankly ahead.

After a time two cheerful women entered. The men greeted them:

"Morning, Mrs. Cockson. Glad to see you're on your feet this merry morning."

"Good morning, good morning, good morning all. You know Mrs. Benson?"

"I don't think I've had that pleasure. Will you join us, Mrs. Benson? I'm in the chair," and he turned and called to the steward: "Boy."

Mr. Pinfold studied this group with benevolence. No one among them would be a Pinfold fan. Presently, at one o'clock, a steward appeared with a gong and Mr. Pinfold followed him submissively down to the dining-saloon.

The Captain's table was laid for seven. The "fiddles" were up and the cloth damped; barely a quarter of the places in the saloon were taken.

Only one other of the Captain's party came to luncheon, a tall young Englishman who fell into easy conversation with Mr. Pinfold, informing him that he was named Glover and was manager of a tea plantation in Ceylon; an idyllic life, as he described it, lived on horse-back with frequent long leave at a golf club. Glover was keen on golf. In order to keep

47

himself in condition for the game on board ship he had a weighted club, its head on a spring, which he swung, he said, a hundred times morning and evening. His cabin, it transpired, was next to Mr. Pinfold's.

"We have to share a bathroom. When do you like your bath?"

Glover's conversation did not demand sharp attention. Mr. Pinfold found himself recalled into a world beyond which he had momentarily wandered, to answer: "Well, really, I hardly ever have a bath at sea. One keeps so clean and I don't like hot salt water. I tried to book a private bathroom. I can't think why."

"There aren't any private baths in this ship."

"So I learned. It seems a very decent sort of ship," said Mr. Pinfold, gazing sadly at his curry, at his swaying glass of wine, at the surrounding deserted table, wishing to be pleasant to Glover.

"Yes. Everyone knows everyone else. The same people travel in her every year. People sometimes complain they feel rather out of things if they aren't regulars."

"I shan't complain," said Mr. Pinfold. "I've been rather ill. I want a quiet time."

"Sorry to hear that. You'll find it quiet enough. Some find it too quiet."

"It can't be too quiet for me," said Mr. Pinfold.

He took rather formal leave of Glover and at once forgot him until, reaching his cabin, he found added to its other noises the strains of a jazz band. Mr. Pinfold stood puzzled. He was not musical. All he knew was that somewhere quite near him a band was playing. Then he remembered.

"It's the golfer," he thought. "That young man next door. He's got a gramophone. What's more," he suddenly observed, "he's got a *dog*." Quite distinctly on the linoleum outside his door, between his door and Glover's, he heard the pattering of a dog's feet. "I bet he's not allowed it. I've never been in a ship where they allowed dogs in the cabins. I daresay he bribed the steward. Anyway, one can't reasonably object. I don't mind. He seemed a very pleasant fellow."

He noticed his grey pills, took one, lay down, opened his book and then to the sound of dance tunes and the snuffling of the dog, he fell asleep once more.

Perhaps he dreamed. He forgot on the instant whatever had happened in the hours between. It

49

was dark. He was awake and there was a very curious scene being played near him; under his feet it seemed. He heard distinctly a clergyman conducting a religious meeting. Mr. Pinfold had no first-hand acquaintance with evangelical practice. His home and his schools had professed a broad-to-high anglicanism. His ideas of noncomformity derived from literature, from Mr. Chadband and Philip Henry Gosse, from charades and from back numbers of *Punch*. The sermon, which was just rising to its peroration, was plainly an expression of that kind of faith, scriptural in diction, emotional in appeal. It was addressed presumably to members of the crew. Male voices sang a hymn which Mr. Pinfold remembered from his nursery where his nanny, like almost all nannies, had been Calvinist: *"Pull for the shore, sailor. Pull for the shore."*

"I want to see Billy alone after you dismiss," said the clergyman. There followed an extempore, rather perfunctory prayer, then a great shuffling of feet and pushing about of chairs; then a hush; then the clergyman, very earnestly: "Well, Billy, what have you got to say to me?" and the unmistakable sound of sobbing.

Mr. Pinfold began to feel uneasy. This was something that was not meant to be overheard.

"Billy, you must tell me yourself. I am not accusing you of anything. I am not putting words into your mouth."

Silence except for sobbing.

"Billy, you know what we talked about last time. Have you done it again? Have you been impure, Billy?"

"Yes, sir. I can't help it, sir."

"God never tempts us beyond our strength, Billy. I've told you that, haven't I? Do you suppose I do not feel these temptations, too, Billy? Very strongly at times. But I resist, don't I? You know I resist, don't I, Billy?"

Mr. Pinfold was horror-struck. He was being drawn into participation in a scene of gruesome indecency. His sticks lay by the bunk. He took the blackthorn and beat strongly on the floor.

"Did you hear anything then, Billy? A knocking. That is God knocking at the door of your soul. He can't come and help you unless you are pure, like me."

This was more than Mr. Pinfold could bear. He

took painfully to his feet, put on his coat, brushed his hair. The voices below him continued:

"I can't help it, sir. I want to be good. I try. I can't."

"You've got pictures of girls stuck up by your bunk, haven't you?"

"Yes, sir."

"Filthy pictures."

"Yes, sir."

"How can you say you want to be good when you keep temptation deliberately before your eyes. I shall come and destroy those pictures."

"No, please, sir. I want them."

Mr. Pinfold hobbled out of his cabin and up to the main deck. The sea was calmer now. More passengers were about in the lounge and the bar. It was half past six. A group were throwing dice for drinks. Mr. Pinfold sat alone and ordered a cocktail. When the steward brought it, he asked: "Does this ship carry a regular chaplain?"

"Oh no, sir. The Captain reads the prayers on Sundays."

"There's a clergyman, then, among the passengers?"

"I haven't seen one, sir. Here's the list."

Mr. Pinfold studied the passenger list. No name bore any prefix indicating Holy Orders. A strange ship, thought Mr. Pinfold, in which laymen were allowed to evangelize a presumably heathen crew; religious mania perhaps on the part of one of the officers.

Waking and sleeping he had lost count of time. It seemed he had been many days at sea in this strange ship. When Glover came into the bar, Mr. Pinfold said affably: "Nice to see you again."

Glover looked slightly startled by this greeting.

"I've been down in my cabin," he said.

"I had to come up. I was embarrassed by that prayer-meeting. Weren't you?"

"Prayer-meeting?" said Glover. "No."

"Right under our feet. Couldn't you hear it?"

"I heard nothing," said Glover.

He began to move away.

"Have a drink," said Mr. Pinfold.

"I won't, thanks. I don't. Have to be careful in a place like Ceylon."

"How's your dog?"

"My dog?"

"Your crypto-dog. The stowaway. Please don't think I'm complaining. I don't mind your dog. Nor your gramophone for that matter."

"But I haven't a dog. I haven't a gramophone."

"Oh well," said Mr. Pinfold huffily. "Perhaps I am mistaken."

If Glover did not wish to confide in him, he would not try to force himself on the young man.

"See you at dinner," said Glover, making off.

He was wearing a dinner jacket, Mr. Pinfold noticed, as were several other passengers. Time to change. Mr. Pinfold went back to his cabin. No sound came now from below; the pseudo-priest and the unchaste seaman had left. But the jazz band was going full blast. So it was not Glover's gramophone. As he changed, Mr. Pinfold considered the matter. During the war he had travelled in troop-ships which were fitted with amplifiers on every deck. Unintelligible alarms and orders had issued from these devices and at certain hours popular music. The *Caliban*, plainly, was equipped in this way. It would be a great nuisance when he began to write. He would have to enquire whether there was some way of cutting it off.

It took him a long time to dress. His fingers were

54

unusually clumsy with studs and tie, and his face in the glass was still blotched and staring. By the time he was ready the gong was sounding for dinner. He did not attempt to wear his evening shoes. Instead he slipped into the soft, fur-lined boots in which he had come aboard. With one hand firmly on the rail, the other on his cane, he made his way laboriously down to the saloon. On the stairs he noticed a bronze plaque recording that this ship had been manned by the Royal Navy during the war and had served in the landing in North Africa and Normandy.

He was first at his table, one of the earliest diners in the ship. He noticed a small dark man in day clothes sitting at a table alone. Then the place began to fill. He watched his fellow passengers in a slightly dazed way. The purser's table, as is common in ships of the kind, had the gayest party, the few girls and young women, the more jovial men from the bar. A plate of soup was set before Mr. Pinfold. Two or three coloured stewards stood together by a service table talking in undertones. Suddenly Mr. Pinfold was surprised to hear from them three obscene epithets spoken in clear English tones. He looked and glared. One of the men immediately slid to his side.

"Yes, sir; something to drink, sir."

There was no hint of mockery in the gentle face, no echo in that soft South Indian accent of the gross tones he had overheard. Baffled, Mr. Pinfold said: "Wine."

"Wine, sir?"

"You have some champagne on board, I suppose?"

"Oh yes sir. Three names. I show list."

"Don't bother about the name. Just bring half a bottle."

Glover came and sat opposite.

"I owe you an apology," said Mr. Pinfold. "It wasn't your gramophone. Part of the naval equipment left over from the war."

"Oh," said Glover. "That was it, was it?"

"It seems the most likely explanation."

"Perhaps it does."

"Very odd language the servants use."

"They're from Travancore."

"No. I mean the way they swear. In front of us, I mean. I daresay they don't mean to be insolent but it shows bad discipline."

"I've never noticed it," said Glover.

He was not at his ease with Mr. Pinfold.

Then the table filled up. Captain Steerforth greeted

them and took his place at the head. He was an un-
remarkable man at first sight. A pretty, youngish
woman introduced as Mrs. Scarfield sat next to Mr.
Pinfold. He explained that he was temporarily a
cripple and could not stand up. "My doctor has
given me some awfully strong pills to take. They
make me feel rather odd. You must forgive me if I'm
a dull companion."

"We're all very dull, I'm afraid," she said. "You're
the writer, aren't you? I'm afraid I never seem to
get any time for reading."

Mr. Pinfold was inured to this sort of conversation but tonight he could not cope. He said: "I wish
I didn't," and turned stupidly to his wine. "She probably thinks I'm drunk," he thought and made an attempt to explain: "They are big grey pills. I don't
know what's in them. I don't believe my doctor does
either. Something new."

"That's always exciting, isn't it?" said Mrs. Scarfield.

Mr. Pinfold despaired and spent the rest of dinner, at which he ate very little, in silence.

The Captain rose, his party with him. Mr. Pinfold,
slow to move, was still in his chair, fumbling for his
stick, when they passed behind him. He got to his

feet. He would have dearly liked to go to his cabin but he was held back, partly by the odd fear that he would be suspected of sea-sickness but more by an odder sentiment, a bond of duty which he conceived held him to Captain Steerforth. It seemed to him that he was in some way under this man's command and that it would be a grave default to leave him until he was dismissed. So, laboriously, he followed them to the lounge and lowered himself into an arm-chair between the Scarfields. They were drinking coffee. He offered them all brandy. They refused and for himself he ordered brandy and *crème de menthe* mixed. As he did so Mr. and Mrs. Scarfield exchanged a glance, which he intercepted, as though to confirm some previous confidence — "My dear, that man next to me, the author, was completely tight." "Are you sure?" "Simply plastered."

Mrs. Scarfield was really extremely pretty, Mr. Pinfold thought. She would not keep that skin long in Burma.

Mr. Scarfield was in the timber trade, teak. His prospects depended less on his own industry and acumen than on the action of politicians. He addressed the little circle on this subject.

"In a democracy," said Mr. Pinfold with more

58

weight than originality, "men do not seek authority so that they may impose a policy. They seek a policy so that they may achieve authority."

He proceeded to illustrate this theme with examples.

At one time or another he had met most of the Government Front Bench. Some were members of Bellamy's whom he knew well. Oblivious of his audience he began to speak of them with familiarity, as he would have done among his friends. The Scarfields again exchanged glances and it occurred to him, too late, that he was not among people who thought it on the whole rather discreditable to know politicians. These people thought he was showing off.

He stopped in the middle of a sentence, silent with shame.

"It must be very exciting to move behind the scenes," said Mrs. Scarfield. "We only know what we see in the papers."

Was there malice behind her smile? At first meeting she had seemed frank and friendly. Mr. Pinfold thought he discovered sly hostility now.

"Oh, I hardly ever read the political columns," he said.

"You don't have to, do you? Getting it all first hand."

There was no doubt in Mr. Pinfold's mind. He had made an ass of himself. Reckless now of his reputation as a good sailor, he attempted a little bow to include the Captain and the Scarfields.

"If you'll excuse me, I think I'll go to my cabin."

He had difficulty getting out of his deep chair, he had difficulty with his stick, he had difficulty keeping his balance. They had barely said "Goodnight," he was still struggling away from them, when something the Captain said made them laugh. Three distinct laughs, all, in Mr. Pinfold's ears, cruelly derisive. On his way out he passed Glover. Moved to explain himself he said: "I don't know anything about politics."

"No?" said Glover.

"Tell them I don't know anything."

"Tell who?"

"The Captain."

"He's just behind you over there."

"Oh well, it doesn't matter."

He hobbled away and looking back from the doors saw Glover talking to the Scarfields. They were ostensibly arranging a four for bridge but Mr. Pinfold knew they had another darker interest — *him.*

It was not yet nine o'clock. Mr. Pinfold undressed. He hung up his clothes, washed and took his pill. There were three tablespoonfuls left in his bottle of sleeping-draught. He decided to try and spend the night without it, to delay anyway until after midnight. The sea was much calmer now; he could lie in bed without rolling. He lay at his ease and began to read one of the novels he had brought on board.

Then, before he had turned a page, the band struck up. This was no wireless performance. It was a living group just under his feet, rehearsing. They were in the same place, as inexplicably audible, as the afternoon Bible class, young, happy people, the party doubtless from the purser's table. Their instruments were drums and rattles and some sort of pipe. The drums and rattles did most of the work. Mr. Pinfold knew nothing of music. It seemed to him that the rhythms they played derived from some very primitive tribe and were of anthropological rather than artistic interest. This guess was confirmed.

"Let's try the Pocoputa Indian one," said the young man who acted, without any great air of authority, as leader.

"Oh not *that*. It's so beastly," said a girl.

"I know," said the leader. "It's the three-eight rhythm. The Gestapo discovered it independently, you know. They used to play it in the cells. It drove the prisoners mad."

"Yes," said another girl. "Thirty-six hours did for anyone. Twelve was enough for most. They could stand any torture but that."

"It drove them absolutely mad." "Raving mad." "Stark, staring mad." "It was the worst torture of all." "The Russians use it now." The voices, some male, some female, all young and eager, came tumbling like puppies. "The Hungarians do it best." "Good old three-eight." "Good old Pocoputa Indians." "They were mad."

"I suppose no one can hear us?" said a sweet girlish voice.

"Don't be so wet, Mimi. Everyone's up on the main deck."

"All right then," said the band leader. "The three-eight rhythm."

And off they went.

The sound throbbed and thrilled in the cabin, which had suddenly become a prison cell. Mr. Pinfold was not one who thought and talked easily to a musical accompaniment. Even in early youth he had sought the night-clubs where there was a bar out of hearing of the band. Friends he had, Roger Stillingfleet among them, to whom jazz was a necessary drug — whether stimulant or narcotic Mr. Pinfold did not know. He preferred silence. The three-eight rhythm was indeed torture to him. He could not read. It was not a quarter of an hour since he had entered the cabin. Unendurable hours lay ahead. He emptied the bottle of sleeping-draught and, to the strains of the jolly young people from the purser's table, fell into unconsciousness.

He awoke before dawn. The bright young people below him had dispersed. The three-eight rhythm was hushed. No shadow passed between the deck-light and the cabin window. But overhead there was turmoil. The crew, or a considerable part of it, was engaged on an operation of dragging the deck with what from the sound of it might have been an enormous chain-harrow, and they were not happy in their work. They were protesting mutinously in their own tongue and the officer in command was roaring back at them in the tones of an old sea-dog: "Get on with it, you black bastards. Get on with it."

The Lascars were not so easily quelled. They shouted back unintelligibly.

"I'll call out the Master-at-Arms," shouted the officer. An empty threat, surely? thought Mr. Pinfold. It was scarcely conceivable that the *Caliban* carried a Master-at-Arms. "By God, I'll shoot the first man of you that moves," said the officer.

The hubbub increased. Mr. Pinfold could almost see the drama overhead, the half-lighted deck, the dark frenzied faces, the solitary bully with the heavy old-fashioned ship's pistol. Then there was a crash, not a shot but a huge percussion of metal as though a hundred pokers and pairs of tongs had fallen into an enormous fender, followed by a wail of agony and a moment of complete silence.

"There," said the officer more in the tones of a nanny than a sea-dog, "just see what you've gone and done now."

Whatever its nature this violent occurrence entirely subdued the passions of the crew. They were docile, ready to do anything to retrieve the disaster. The only sounds now were the officer's calmer orders and the whimpering of the injured man.

"Steady there. Easy does it. You, cut along to the sick-bay and get the surgeon. You, go up and report to the bridge . . . "

For a long time, two hours perhaps, Mr. Pinfold lay in his bunk listening. He was able to hear quite distinctly not only what was said in his immediate vicinity, but elsewhere. He had the light on, now, in his cabin, and as he gazed at the complex of tubes and wires which ran across his ceiling, he realised that they must form some kind of general junction in the system of communication. Through some trick or fault or war-time survival everything spoken in the executive quarters of the ship was transmitted to him. A survival seemed the most likely explanation. Once during the blitz in London he had been given an hotel bed-room which had been hastily vacated by a visiting allied statesman. When he lifted the telephone to order his breakast, he had found himself talking on a private line direct to the Cabinet Office. Something of that kind must have happened in the *Caliban*. When she was a naval vessel this cabin had no doubt been the office of some operational headquarters and when she was handed back to her owners and re-adapted for passenger service, the engineers had neglected to disconnect it. That alone could explain the voices which now kept him informed of every stage of the incident.

The wounded man seemed to have got himself entangled in some kind of web of metal. Various unsuccessful and agonizing attempts were made to extricate him. Finally the decision was taken to cut him out. The order once given was carried out with surprising speed but the contraption, whatever it was, was ruined in the process and was finally dragged across the deck and thrown overboard. The victim continuously sobbed and whimpered. He was taken to the sick-bay and put in charge of a kind but not, it appeared, very highly qualified nurse. "You must be brave," she said. "I will say the rosary for you. You must be brave," while the wireless telegraphist got into touch with a hospital ashore and was given instructions in first aid. The ship's surgeon never appeared. Details of treatment were dictated from the shore and passed to the sick-bay. The last words Mr. Pinfold heard from the bridge were Captain Steerforth's "I'm not going to be bothered with a sick man on board. We'll have to signal a passing home-bound ship and have him transferred."

Part of the treatment prescribed by the hospital

was a sedative injection and as this spread its relief over the unhappy Lascar, Mr. Pinfold too grew drowsy until finally he fell asleep to the sound of the nurse murmuring the Angelic Salutation.

He was awakened by the coloured cabin steward bringing him tea.

"Very disagreeable business that last night," said Mr. Pinfold.

"Yes, sir."

"How is the poor fellow?"

"Eight o'clock, sir."

"Have they managed to get into touch with a ship to take him off?"

"Yes, sir. Breakfast eight-thirty, sir."

Mr. Pinfold drank his tea. He felt disinclined to get up. The intercommunication system was silent. He picked up his book and began to read. Then with a click the voices began again.

Captain Steerforth seemed to be addressing a deputation of the crew. "I want you to understand," he was saying, "that a great quantity of valuable metal was sacrificed last night for the welfare of a single seaman. That metal was pure *copper*. One of the most valuable metals in the world. Mind you I don't regret the sacrifice and I am sure the Company will approve my action. But I want you all to appreciate that only in a British ship would such a thing be done. In the ship of any other nationality it would have been the seaman not the metal that was cut up. You know that as well as I do. Don't forget it. And another thing, instead of taking the man with us to Port Said and an Egyptian hospital, I had him carefully transhipped and he is now on his way to England. He couldn't have been treated more handsomely if he'd been a director of the Company. I know the hospital he's going to; it's a sweet, pretty place. It's the place all seamen long to go to. He'll have the best attention there and live, if he does live, in the greatest comfort. That's the kind of ship this is. Nothing is too good for the men who serve in her."

The meeting seemed to disperse. There was a shuffling and muttering and presently a woman spoke. It was a voice which was soon to become familiar to Mr. Pinfold. To all men and women there is some sound — grating, perhaps, or rustling, or strident, deep or shrill, a note of inflection of speech — which causes peculiar pain; which literally "makes the hair stand on end" or metaphorically "sets the teeth on edge"; something which Dr. Drake would have called an "allergy." Such was this woman's voice. It clearly did not affect the Captain in this way but to Mr. Pinfold it was excruciating.

"Well," said this voice. "That should teach them not to grumble."

"Yes," said Captain Steerforth. "We've settled that little mutiny, I think. We shouldn't have any trouble now."

"Not till the next time," said the cynical woman. "What a contemptible exhibition that man made of himself — crying like a child. Thank God we've seen the last of him. I liked your touch about the sweet, pretty hospital."

"Yes. They little know the hell-spot I've sent him to. Spoiling my copper, indeed. He'll soon wish he were in Port Said."

And the woman laughed odiously. "Soon wish he was dead," she said.

There was a click — someone seemed to be in control of the apparatus, Mr. Pinfold thought — and two passengers were speaking. They seemed to be elderly, military gentlemen.

"I think the passengers should be told," one said.

"Yes, we ought to call a meeting. It's the sort of thing that so often passes without proper recognition. We ought to pass a vote of thanks."

"A ton of copper, you say?"

"Pure copper, cut up and chucked overboard. It makes one proud of the British service."

The voices ceased and Mr. Pinfold lay wondering about this meeting; was it his duty to attend and report what he knew of the true characters of the Captain and his female associate? The difficulty, of course, would be to prove his charges; to explain satisfactorily how he came to overhear the Captain's secret.

Soft music filled the cabin, an oratorio sung by a great but distant choir. "That must be a gramophone record," thought Mr. Pinfold. "Or the wireless. They can't be performing this on board." Then he slept for some time, until he was woken by a change of music. The bright young people were at it again with their Pocoputa Indian three-eight rhythm. Mr. Pinfold looked at his watch. Eleven-thirty. Time to get up.

As he laboriously shaved and dressed, he reasoned closely about his situation. Now that he knew of the intercommunication system, it was plain to him that the room used by this band might be anywhere in the ship. The prayer-meeting too. It had seemed odd at the time that the quiet voice had come so

clearly through the floor; that they had been audible
to him and not to Glover. That was now explained.
But he was puzzled by the irregularity, by the
changes of place, the clicking on and off. It was im-
probable that anyone at a switchboard was direct-
ing the annoyances into his cabin. It was certain that
the Captain would not deliberately broadcast his
private and compromising conversations. Mr. Pinfold wished he knew more of the mechanics of the
thing. He remembered that in London just after the
war, when everything was worn out, telephones used
sometimes to behave in this erratic way; the line
would go dead; then crackle; then, when the tangled
wire was given a twist and a jerk, normal conversation was rejoined. He supposed that somewhere over
his head, in the ventilation shaft probably, there
were a number of frayed and partly disconnected
wires which every now and then with the movement of the ship came into contact and so established
communication now with one, now with another
part of the ship.

Before leaving his cabin he considered his box of
pills. He was not well. Much was wrong with him,
he felt, beside lameness. Dr. Drake did not know
about the sleeping-draught. It might be that the

pills, admittedly new and pretty strong, warred with the bromide and chloral; perhaps with gin and brandy too. Well, the sleeping-draught was finished. He would try the pills once or twice more. He swallowed one and crept up to the main deck.

Here there was light and liveliness, a glitter of cool sunshine and a brisk breeze. The young people had abandoned the concert in the short time it had taken Mr. Pinfold to climb the stairs. They were on the after deck playing quoits and shuffle-board and watching one another play, laughing boisterously as the ship rolled and jostled them against one another. Mr. Pinfold leant on the rail and looked down, thinking it odd that such healthy-seeming, good-natured creatures should rejoice in the music of the Pocoputa Indians. Glover stood by himself in the stern swinging his golf club. On the sunny side of the main deck the older passengers sat wrapped in rugs, some with popular biographies, some with knitting. The young Burmese paced together in pairs, uniformly and neatly dressed in blazers and pale fawn trousers, like officers waiting to fall in at a battalion parade.

Mr. Pinfold sought the military gentlemen whose ill-informed eulogies of the Captain he believed it to be his duty to correct. From the voices, elderly, precise, conventional, he had formed a clear idea of their appearance. They were Major-Generals, retired now. They had been gallant young regimental officers — line-cavalry probably — in 1914 and had commanded brigades at the end of that war. They had passed at the Staff College and waited patiently for another battle only to find in 1939 that they were passed over for active command. But they had served loyally in offices, done their turn at fire-watching, gone short of whisky and razor-blades. Now they could just afford an inexpensive winter cruise every other year, admirable old men in their way. He did not find them on deck or in any of the public rooms.

As noon was sounded there was a movement towards the bar for the announcement of the ship's run and the result of the sweepstake. Scarfield was the winner of a modest prize. He ordered drinks for all in sight including Mr. Pinfold. Mrs. Scarfield stood near him and Mr. Pinfold said: "I say I'm afraid I was an awful bore last night."

"Were you?" she said. "Not while you were with us."

"All that nonsense I talked about politics. It's

73

those pills I have to take. They make me feel rather
odd."

"I'm sorry about that," said Mrs. Scarfield, "but I
assure you, you didn't bore *us* in the least. I was
fascinated."

Mr. Pinfold looked hard at her but could detect
no hint of irony. "Anyway I shan't hold forth like
that again."

"Please do."

The ladies who had been identified as Mrs. Benson and Mrs. Cockson were in the same chairs as on
the day before. They liked their glass, that pair,
thought Mr. Pinfold with approval; good sorts. He
greeted them. He greeted anyone who caught his
eye. He was feeling very much better.

One figure alone remained aloof from the general
conviviality, the dark little man whom Mr. Pinfold
had noticed dining alone.

Presently the steward passed by, tapping his little
musical gong, and Mr. Pinfold followed the company down to luncheon. Knowing what he did of
Captain Steerforth's character, Mr. Pinfold found it
rather repugnant to sit at the table with him. He
gave him a perfunctory nod and addressed himself
to Glover.

"Noisy night, wasn't it?"

"Oh," said Glover, "I didn't hear anything."

"You must sleep very sound."

"As a matter of fact, I didn't. I usually do, but I am not getting the exercise I'm used to. I was awake half the night."

"And you didn't hear the accident?"

"No."

"Accident?" said Mrs. Scarfield, overhearing. "Was there an accident last night, Captain?"

"No one told me of one," said Captain Steerforth blandly.

"The villain," thought Mr. Pinfold. "Remorseless, treacherous, lecherous, kindless villain," for though Captain Steerforth had shown no other symptoms of lechery, Mr. Pinfold knew instinctively that his relations with the harsh-voiced woman — stewardess, secretary, passenger, whatever she might be — were grossly erotic.

"What accident, Mr. Pinfold?" asked Mrs. Scarfield.

"Perhaps I was mistaken," said Mr. Pinfold stiffly. "I often am."

There was another couple at the Captain's table. They had been there the night before, had been part

75

of the group in which Mr. Pinfold had talked so injudiciously, but he had barely noticed them; a pleasant, middle-aged nondescript, rather rich-looking couple, not English, Dutch perhaps or Scandinavian. The woman now leant across and said in thick, rather arch tones:

"There are two books of yours in the ship's library, I find."

"Ah."

"I have taken one. It is named *The Last Card*."

"*The Lost Chord*," said Mr. Pinfold.

"Yes. It is a humorous book, yes?"

"Some people have suggested as much."

"I find it so. It is not your suggestion also? I think you have a peculiar sense of humour, Mr. Pinfold."

"Ah."

"That is what you are known for, yes, your peculiar sense of humour?"

"Perhaps."

"May I have it after you?" asked Mrs. Scarfield. "Everyone says I have a peculiar sense of humour too."

"But not so peculiar as Mr. Pinfold?"

"That remains to be seen," said Mrs. Scarfield.

"I think you're embarrassing the author," said Mr. Scarfield.

"I expect he's used to it," she said.

"He takes it all with his peculiar sense of humour," said the foreign lady.

"If you'll excuse me," said Mr. Pinfold, struggling to rise.

"You see he is embarrassed."

"No," said the foreign lady, "it is his humour. He is going to make notes of us. You see, we shall all be in a humorous book."

As Mr. Pinfold rose, he gazed towards the little dark man at his solitary table. That is where he should have been, he thought. The last sound he heard as he left the dining-saloon was merry young laughter from the purser's table.

Since he left it not much more than an hour before, the cabin had been tidied and the bed clothes stretched taut, hospital-like, across the bunk. He took off his coat and his soft boots, lit a cigar and lay down. He had barely eaten at all that day but he was not hungry. He blew smoke up towards the wires and pipes on the ceiling and wondered how without offence he could escape from the Captain's table to sit and eat alone, silent and untroubled, like that clever, dark enviable little fellow, and as though in response to these thoughts the device overhead clicked into life and he heard this very subject being debated by the two old soldiers.

"My dear fellow, *I* don't care a damn."

"No, of course you don't. Nor do I. All the same I think it very decent of him to mention it."

"*Very* decent. What did he say exactly?"

"Said he was very sorry he hadn't room for you and me and my missus. The table only takes six passengers. Well, he had to have the Scarfields."

"Yes, of course. He *had* to have the Scarfields."

"Yes, he had to have them. Then there's the Norwegian couple — foreigners, you know."

"Distinguished foreigners."

"Got to be civil to them. Well that makes four. Then if you please, he got an order from the Company to take this fellow Pinfold. So he only had one place. Knew he couldn't separate you and me and the missus, so he asked that decent young fellow — the one with the uncle in Liverpool."

"Has he got an uncle in Liverpool?"

"Yes, yes. That's why he asked him."

"But why did he ask Pinfold?"

78

"Company's orders. *He* didn't want him."

"No, no, of course not."

"If you ask me, Pinfold drinks."

"Yes, so I have always heard."

"I saw him come on board. He was tight then. In a beastly state."

"He's been in a beastly state ever since."

"He says it's pills."

"No, no, drink. I've seen better men than Pinfold go that way."

"Wretched business. He shouldn't have come."

"If you ask me he's been *sent* on this ship as a *cure*."

"Ought to have someone to look after him."

"Have you noticed that little dark chap who sits alone? I shouldn't be surprised if *he* wasn't keeping an eye on him."

"A male nurse?"

"A warder more likely."

"Put on him by his missus without his knowing?"

"That's my appreciation of the situation."

The voices of the two old gossips faded and fell silent. Mr. Pinfold lay smoking, without resentment. It was the sort of thing one expected to have said behind one's back — the sort of thing one said about

79

other people. It was slightly unnerving to overhear
it. The idea of his wife setting a spy on him was
amusing. He would write and tell her. The question
of his drunkenness interested him more. Perhaps he
did give that impression. Perhaps on that first evening at sea — how long ago was that now? — when
he had talked politics after dinner, perhaps he *had*
drunk too much. He had had too much of something
certainly, pills or sleeping-draught or liquor. Well,
the sleeping-draught was finished. He resolved to
take no more pills. He would stick to wine
and a cocktail or two and a glass of brandy after
dinner and soon he would be well and active
once more.

He had reached the last inch of his cigar, a large
one, an hour's smoking, when his reverie was inter-
rupted from the Captain's cabin.

The doxy was there. In her harsh voice she said,
"You've got to teach him a lesson."

"I will."

"A *good* lesson."

"Yes."

"One he won't forget."

"Bring him in."

There was a sound of scuffling and whimpering, a sound rather like that of the wounded seaman whom Mr. Pinfold had heard that morning — which morning? — one morning of this disturbing voyage. It seemed that a prisoner was being dragged into the Captain's presence.

"Tie him to the chair," said the leman, and Mr. Pinfold at once thought of *King Lear:* "Bind fast his corky arms." Who said that? Goneril? Regan? Perhaps neither of them. Cornwall? It was a man's voice, surely? in the play. But it was the voice of the woman, or what passed as a woman, here. Addict of nicknames as he was, Mr. Pinfold there and then dubbed her "Goneril."

"All right," said Captain Steerforth, "you can leave him to me."

"And to me," said Goneril.

Mr. Pinfold was not abnormally squeamish nor had his life been particularly sheltered, but he had no experience of personal, physical cruelty and no liking for its portrayal in books or films. Now, lying in his spruce cabin in this British ship, in the early afternoon, a few yards distant from Glover and the Scarfields, Mrs. Benson and Mrs. Cockson, he was the horrified witness of a scene which might have come straight from the kind of pseudo-American thriller he most abhorred.

There were three people in the Captain's cabin, Steerforth, Goneril and their prisoner, who was one of the coloured stewards. Proceedings began with a form of trial. Goneril gave her evidence, vindictively but precisely accusing the man of an attempted sexual offence against her.

It sounded to Mr. Pinfold rather a strong case. Knowing the ambiguous position which the accuser held in the ship, remembering the gross language he had overheard in the dining saloon and the heavy, unhealthy discourse of the preacher, Mr. Pinfold considered the incident he heard described exactly the sort of thing he would expect to happen in this beastly ship. Guilty, he thought.

"Guilty," said the Captain and at the word Goneril vented a hiss of satisfaction and anticipation. Slowly and deliberately, as the ship steamed south with its commonplace load of passengers, the Captain and his leman with undisguised erotic enjoyment settled down to torture their prisoner.

Mr. Pinfold could not surmise what form the torture took. He could only listen to the moans and sobs of the victim and the more horrific, ecstatic, orgiastic cries of Goneril:

"More. More. Again. Again. Again. You haven't had anything yet, you beast. Give him some more, more, more, more."

Mr. Pinfold could not endure it. He must stop this outrage at once. He lurched from his bunk, but even as he felt for his boots, silence fell in the Captain's cabin and a suddenly sobered Goneril said: "That's enough."

Not a sound came from the victim. After a long pause Captain Steerforth said: "If you ask me, it's too much."

"He's shamming," said Goneril without conviction.

"He's dead," said the Captain.

"Well," said Goneril. "What are you going to do about it?"

"Untie him."

"I'm not going to touch him. I never touched him. It was all *you*."

Mr. Pinfold stood in his cabin, just as, no doubt, the Captain was standing in his, uncertain what to do, and as he hesitated he realized through his horror that the pains in his legs had suddenly entirely ceased. He rose on his toes; he bent his knees. He

83

was cured. It was the way in which these attacks of his always came and went, quite unpredictably. In spite of his agitation he had room in his mind to consider whether perhaps they were nervous in origin, whether the shock he had just endured might not have succeeded where the grey pills had failed; whether he had not been healed by the steward's agony. It was a hypothesis which momentarily distracted him from the murderer above.

Presently he turned to listen to them.

"As master of the ship I shall make out a death-certificate and have him put overboard after dark."

"How about the surgeon?"

"He must sign too. The first thing is to get the body into the sick-bay. We don't want any more trouble with the men. Get Margaret."

The situation, as Mr. Pinfold saw it, was appalling but it did not call for action.

Whatever had to be done, need not be done now. He could not burst alone into the Captain's cabin and denounce him. What was the proper procedure, if any existed, for putting a Captain in irons in his own ship? He would have to take advice. The military men, that sage, authoritative couple, were the obvious people. He would find them and explain the situation. They would know what to do. A report must be made, he assumed, depositions taken. Where? At the first consulate they came to, at Port Said; or should they wait until they reached a British port? Those old campaigners would know.

Meanwhile Margaret, the kind nurse, a sort of Cordelia, seemed to have charge of the body. "Poor boy, poor boy," she was saying. "Look at these ghastly marks. You can't say these are 'natural causes.'"

"That's what the Captain says," said a new voice, the ship's surgeon's presumably. "I take my orders from him. There's a lot goes on aboard this ship that I don't like. The best you can do, young lady, is to see nothing, hear nothing and say nothing."

"But the poor boy. He must have suffered so."

"Natural causes," said the doctor. And then there was silence.

Mr. Pinfold removed his soft boots and put on shoes. He propped his two sticks in a corner of the wardrobe. "I shan't need those again," he reflected, little knowing what the coming days had in store, and walked almost blithely to the main deck.

No one was about except two Lascars, slung overhead, painting the davits. It was half past three, a time when all the passengers were in their cabins. Like a lark on a battle-field Mr. Pinfold's spirits rose, free and singing. He rejoiced in his power to walk. He walked round the ship, again and again, up and down. Was it possible, in this bright and peaceful scene, to believe in the abomination that lurked up there, just overhead, behind the sparkling paint? Could he possibly be mistaken? He had never seen Goneril. He barely knew the Captain's voice. Could he really identify it? Was it not possible that what he had heard was a piece of acting — a charade of the bright young people's? a broadcast from London?

Wishful thinking, perhaps, born on the exhilaration of sun and sea and wind and his own new-found health?

Time alone would show.

◄| 4 |►

The Hooligans

THAT EVENING Mr. Pinfold felt the renewal of health and cheerfulness and clarity of mind greater, it seemed to him, than he had known for weeks. He looked at his hands, which for days now had been blotched with crimson; now they were clear and his face in the glass had lost its congested, mottled hue. He dressed more deftly and as he dressed the wireless in his cabin came into action.

"This is the B.B.C. Third Programme. Here is Mr. Clutton-Cornforth to speak on Aspects of Orthodoxy in Contemporary Letters."

Mr. Pinfold had known Clutton-Cornforth for thirty years. He was now the editor of a literary weekly, an ambitious, obsequious fellow. Mr. Pinfold had no curiosity about his opinions on any subject. He wished there were a way of switching off the fluting, fruity voice. He tried instead to disregard it until, just as he was leaving, he was recalled by the sound of his own name.

"Gilbert Pinfold," he heard, "poses a precisely antithetical problem, or, should we say? the same problem in antithetical form. The basic qualities of a Pinfold novel seldom vary and may be enumerated thus: conventionality of plot; falseness of characterization; morbid sentimentality; gross and hackneyed farce, alternating with grosser and more hackneyed melodrama; cloying religiosity, which will be found tedious or blasphemous according as the reader shares or repudiates his doctrinal preconceptions; an adventitious and offensive sensuality that is clearly introduced for commercial motives. All this is presented in a style which, when it varies from the trite, lapses into positive illiteracy."

Really, thought Mr. Pinfold, this was not like the Third Programme; it was not at all like Algernon Clutton-Cornforth. "My word," he thought, "I'll give that booby such a kick on the sit-upon next time I see him waddling up the steps of the London Library."

"Indeed," continued Clutton-Cornforth, "if one is asked — and one *is* often asked — to give one name which typifies all that is decadent in contemporary literature, one can answer without hesitation — Gilbert Pinfold. I now turn from him to the equally deplorable but more interesting case of a writer often associated with him — Roger Stillingfleet."

Here, by a quirk of the apparatus, Clutton-Cornforth was cut off and succeeded by a female singer:

> I'm Gilbert, the filbert,
> The knut with the K,
> The pride of Piccadilly
> The blasé roué . . .

Mr. Pinfold left his cabin. He met the steward on his rounds with the dinner-gong and ascended to the main deck. He stepped out into the wind, leaned briefly on the rail, looked down into the surge of lighted water. The music rejoined him there, emanating from somewhere quite near where he stood.

> For Gilbert, the filbert,
> The Colonel of the Knuts.

Other people in the ship were listening to the wireless. Other people, probably, had heard Clutton-Cornforth's diatribe. Well, he was accustomed to

89

criticism (though not from Clutton-Cornforth). He could take it. He only hoped no one bored him by talking about it; particularly not that Norwegian woman at the Captain's table.

Mr. Pinfold's feelings towards the Captain had moderated in the course of the afternoon. As to whether the man were guilty of murder or no, his judgment was suspended, but the fact of his having fallen under a cloud, of Mr. Pinfold's possession of secret knowledge which might or might not bring him to ruin, severed the bond of loyalty which had previously bound them. Mr. Pinfold felt disposed to tease the Captain a little.

Accordingly at dinner, when they were all seated, and he had ordered himself a pint of champagne, he turned the conversation rather abruptly to the subject of murder.

"Have you ever actually met a murderer?" he asked Glover.

Glover had. In his tea garden a trusted foreman had hacked his wife to pieces.

"I expect he smiled a good deal, didn't he?" asked Mr. Pinfold.

"Yes, as a matter of fact he did. Always a most cheerful chap. He went off to be hanged laughing away with his brothers as though it was no end of a joke."

"*Exactly.*"

Mr. Pinfold stared full in the eyes of the smiling Captain. Was there any sign of alarm in that broad, plain face?

"Have *you* ever known a murderer, Captain Steerforth?"

Yes, when he first went to sea, Captain Steerforth had been in a ship with a stoker who killed another with a shovel. But they brought it in that the man was insane, affected by the heat of the stoke-hold.

"In my country in the forests in the long winter often the men become drunken and fight and sometimes they kill one another. Is not hanging in my country for such things. Is a case for the doctor we think."

"If you ask me all murderers are mad," said Scarfield.

"And always smiling," said Mr. Pinfold. "That's the only way you can tell them — by their inevitable good humour."

"This stoker wasn't very cheerful. Surly fellow as I remember him."

"Ah, but he was mad."

"Goodness," said Mrs. Scarfield, "what a morbid subject. However did we get onto it?"

"Not so morbid by half as Clutton-Cornforth," said Mr. Pinfold rather truculently.

"Who?" asked Mrs. Scarfield.

"As what?" asked the Norwegian woman.

Mr. Pinfold looked from face to face round the table. Clearly no one had heard the broadcast.

"Oh," he said, "if you don't know about him, the less said the better."

"Do tell," said Mrs. Scarfield.

"No, really, it's nothing."

She gave a little shrug of disappointment and turned her pretty face towards the Captain.

Later Mr. Pinfold tried to raise the topic of burial at sea, but this was not taken up with any enthusiasm. Mr. Pinfold had devoted some thought to the matter during the late afternoon. Glover had said that the stewards came from Travancore, in which case there was a good chance of their being Christians of one or other of the ancient rites that prevailed in that complex culture. They would insist on some religious observance for one of their number. If he wished to avert suspicion, the Captain could not bundle the body overboard secretly. Once in a

92

troop-ship Mr. Pinfold had assisted at the committal
to the sea of one of his troop who shot himself. The
business, he remembered, took some time. Last Post
had been sounded. Mr. Pinfold rather thought the
ship had hove-to. In the *Caliban* the sports deck
seemed the most likely place for the ceremony. Mr.
Pinfold would keep watch. If the night passed without incident, Captain Steerforth would stand ac-
quitted.

That evening, as on the evening before, Captain
Steerforth played bridge. He smiled continuously
rubber after rubber. Early hours were kept in the
Caliban. The bar shut at half past ten, lights began
to be turned off and ash trays emptied; the passengers went to their cabins. Mr. Pinfold saw
the last of them go below, then went aft to a seat
overlooking the sports deck. It was very cold.
He went down to his cabin for an overcoat. It was
warm there and welcoming. It occurred to him,
he could keep his vigil perfectly well below deck.
When the engines stopped, he would know that
the game was on. The last faint cobwebs of his
sleeping-draught had now been swept up. He was
wide awake. Without undressing he lay on his bunk
with a novel.

93

Time passed. No sound came through the inter-communication; the engines beat regularly, the plates and panelling creaked; the low hum of the ventilator filled the cabin.

There were no funeral obsequies, no panegyric; no dirge on board the *Caliban* that night. Instead there was enacted on the deck immediately outside Mr. Pinfold's window a dramatic cycle lasting five hours — six? Mr. Pinfold did not notice the time at which the disturbance began — of which he was the solitary audience. Had it appeared behind footlights on a real stage, Mr. Pinfold would have condemned it as grossly overplayed.

There were two chief actors, juvenile leads, one of whom was called Fosker; the other, the leader, was nameless. They were drunk when they first arrived and presumably carried a bottle from which they often swigged, for the long hours of darkness were of no avail in sobering them. They raged more and more furiously until their final lapse into inco-herence. By their voices they seemed to be gentle-men of a sort. Fosker, Mr. Pinfold was pretty sure, had been in the jazz band; he thought he had noticed him in the lounge after dinner, amusing the girls, tall, very young, shabby, shady, vivacious, bohemian, with long hair, a moustache and the beginning of side-whiskers. There was something in him of the dissolute law students and government clerks of mid-Victorian fiction. Something too of the young men who had now and then crossed his path during the war — the sort of subaltern who was disliked in his regiment and got himself posted to S.O.E. When Mr. Pinfold came to consider the matter at leisure he could not explain to himself how he had formed so full an impression during a brief, incurious glance, or why Fosker, if he were what he seemed, should be travelling to the East in such incongruous company. The image of him, however, remained sharp-cut as a cameo. The second, dominant young man was a voice only; rather a pleasant well-bred voice for all its vile utterances.

"He's gone to bed," said Fosker.

"We'll soon get him out," said the pleasant well-bred voice.

"Music."

"Music."

> *I'm Gilbert, the filbert,*
> *The knut with the K.*
> *The pride of Piccadilly,*
> *The blasé roué.*

95

> *Oh Hades, the ladies*
> *Who leave their wooden huts*
> *For Gilbert, the filbert,*
> *The Colonel of the Knuts.*

"Come on, Gilbert. Time to leave your wooden hut."

Damned impudence, thought Mr. Pinfold. Oafs, bores.

"D'you think he's enjoying this?"

"He's got a most peculiar sense of humour? He's a most peculiar man. Queer, aren't you, Gilbert? Come out of your wooden hut, you old queer."

Mr. Pinfold drew the wooden shutter across his window but the noise outside was undiminished.

"He thinks that'll keep us out. It won't, Gilbert. We aren't going to climb through the window, you know. We shall come in at the door and then, by God, you're going to cop it. Now he's locked the door." Mr. Pinfold had done no such thing. "Not very brave, is he? Locking himself in. Gilbert doesn't want to be whipped."

"But he's going to be whipped."

"Oh yes, he's going to be whipped all right."

Mr. Pinfold decided on action. He put on his dressing gown, took his blackthorn, and left his

96

cabin. The door which led out to the deck was some way down the corridor. The voices of the two hooligans followed him as he went to it. He thought he knew the Fosker type, the aggressive underdog, vainglorious in drink, very easily put in his place. He pushed open the heavy door and stepped resolutely into the wind. The deck was quite empty. For the length of the ship the damp planks shone in the lamp-light. From above came shrieks of laughter.

"No, no, Gilbert, you can't catch us that way. Go back to your little hut, Gilbert. We'll come for you when we want you. Better lock the door."

Mr. Pinfold returned to his cabin. He did not lock the door. He sat, stick in hand, listening.

The two young men conferred.

"We'd better wait till he goes to sleep."

"Then we'll pounce."

"He doesn't seem very sleepy."

"Let's get the girls to sing him to sleep. Come on, Margaret, give Gilbert a song."

"Aren't you being rather beastly?" The girl's voice was clear and sober.

"No, of course not. It's all a joke. Gilbert's a sport. Gilbert's enjoying it as much as we are. He often did this sort of thing when he was our age — singing ridiculous songs outside men's rooms at Oxford. He made a row outside the Dean's rooms. That's why he got sent down. He accused the Dean of the most disgusting practices. It was all a great joke."

"Well, if you're sure he doesn't mind . . . "

Two girls began singing very prettily.

> *When first I saw Mabel* — they sang —
> *In her fair Russian sable*
> *I knew she was able*
> *To satisfy me.*
> *Her manners were careless . . .*

The later lines of the song — one well-known to Mr. Pinfold — are verbally bawdy, but as they rose now on the passionless, true voices of the girls, they were purged and sweetened; they floated over the seat in perfect innocence. The girls sang this and other airs. They sang for a long time. They sang intermittently throughout the night's disturbances, but they were powerless to soothe Mr. Pinfold. He sat wide awake with his stick to deal with intruders.

Presently the father of the nameless young man came to join them. He was, it appeared, one of the Generals.

"Go to bed, you two," he said. "You're making an infernal nuisance of yourselves."

"We're only mocking Pinfold. He's a beastly man."

"That's no reason to wake up the whole ship."

"He's a Jew."

"Is he? Are you sure? I never heard that."

"Of course he is. He came to Lychpole in 1937 with the German refugees. He was called Peinfeld then."

"We're out for Peinfeld's blood," said the pleasant voice. "We want to beat hell out of him."

"You don't really mind, do you, sir," said Fosker, "if we beat hell out of him."

"What's wrong with the fellow particularly?"

"He's got a dozen pairs of shoes in his little hut, all beautifully polished in wooden trees."

"He sits at the Captain's table."

"He's taken the only bathroom near our cabin. I tried to use it tonight and the steward said it was private, for Mr. Pinfold."

"Mr. Peinfeld."

"I hate him. I hate him. I hate him. I hate him. I hate him," said Fosker. "I've got my own score to settle with him for what he did to Hill."

"That farmer who shot himself?"

"Hill was a decent, old-fashioned yeoman. The salt of the country. Then this Peinfeld came and bought up the property. The Hills had farmed it for generations. They were thrown out. That's why Hill hanged himself."

"Well," said the General. "You won't do any good by shouting outside his window."

"We're going to do more than that. We're going to give him the hiding of his life."

"Yes, you could do that, of course."

"You leave him to us."

"I'm certainly not going to stay up here and be a witness. He's just the sort of fellow to take legal action."

"He'd be far too ashamed. Can't you see the headlines? 'Novelist whipped in liner.'"

"I don't suppose he'd care a damn. Fellows like that live on publicity." Then the General changed his tone. "All the same," he said wistfully, "I wish I was young enough to help. Good luck to you. Give it to him good and strong. Only remember; if there's trouble, *I* know nothing about it."

The girls sang. The youths drank. Presently the mother came to plead. She spoke in yearning tones

100

that reminded Mr. Pinfold of his deceased Anglican aunts.

"I can't sleep," she said. "You know I can never sleep when you're in this state. My son, I beg you to go to bed. Mr. Fosker, how can you lead him into this escapade? Margaret, darling, what are you doing here at this time of night? *Please* go to your cabin, child."

"It's only a joke, Mama."

"I very much doubt whether Mr. Pinfold thinks it a joke."

"I hate him," said her son.

"Hate?" said the mother. "Hate? Why do all you young people *hate* so much. What has come over the world? You were not brought up to *hate*. Why do you hate Mr. Pinfold?"

"I have to share a cabin with Fosker. That swine has a cabin to himself."

"I expect he paid for it."

"Yes, with the money he cheated Hill out of."

"He behaved badly to Hill certainly. But he isn't used to country ways. I've not met him, though we have lived so near all these years. I think perhaps he rather looks down on all of us. We aren't so clever as

101

he, nor as rich. But that's no reason to *hate* him."

At this the son broke into a diatribe in the course of which he and Fosker were left alone. There had been an element of jollity in the air at the beginning of their demonstration. Now they were possessed by hatred, repeating and elaborating a ferocious, rambling denunciation full of obscenities. The eviction of Hill and responsibility for his suicide were the chief recurring charges but interspersed with them were other accusations. Mr. Pinfold, they said, had let his mother die in destitution. He was ashamed of her because she was an illiterate immigrant, had refused to help her or go near her, had let her die alone, uncared for, had not attended her pauper's funeral. Mr. Pinfold had shirked in the war. He had used it as an opportunity to change his name and pass himself off as an Englishman, to make friends with people who did not know his origin, to get into Bellamy's Club. Mr. Pinfold had in some way been implicated in the theft of a moonstone. He had paid a large sum of money to sit at the Captain's table. Mr. Pinfold typified the decline of England, or rural England in particular. He was a reincarnation (Mr. Pinfold, not they, drew the analogy) of the "new men" of the Tudor period who had

102

despoiled the Church and the peasantry. His religious profession was humbug, assumed in order to ingratiate himself with the aristocracy. Mr. Pinfold was a sodomite. Mr. Pinfold must be chastened and chastised.

The night wore on, the charges became wilder and wider, the threats more bloody. The two young men were like prancing savages working themselves into a frenzy of blood-lust. Mr. Pinfold awaited their attack and prepared for it. He made an operational plan. They would come through the door singly. The cabin was not spacious but there was room to swing a stick. He turned out the light and stood by the door. The young men, coming suddenly into the dark from the lighted corridor, would not know where to lay hands on him. He would fell the first with his blackthorn, then change this weapon for the Malacca cane. The second young man no doubt would stumble over his fallen friend. Mr. Pinfold would then turn on the light and carefully thrash him. They were far too drunk to be really dangerous. Mr. Pinfold was quite confident of the outcome. He awaited them calmly.

The incantations were rising to a climax.

"Now's the time. Ready, Fosker?"

"Ready."

"In we go then."

"You first, Fosker."

Mr. Pinfold stood ready. He was glad that Fosker should be the man to be painlessly stunned; the instigator, the man to receive full punishment. There was justice in that order.

Then came anticlimax. "I can't get in," said Fosker. "The bastard has locked the door."

Mr. Pinfold had not locked the door. Moreover Fosker had not tried it. There had been no movement of the handle. Fosker was afraid.

"Go on. What are you waiting for?"

"I tell you he's locked us out."

"That's torn it."

Crestfallen, the two returned to the deck.

"We've got to get him. We must get him tonight," said the one who was not Fosker, but the fire had gone out of him and he added: "I feel awfully sick suddenly."

"Better put it off for tonight."

"I feel frightful. Oh!"

There followed the ghastly sounds of vomiting and then a whimper; the same abject sound that seemed to re-echo through the *Caliban*, the sob of the injured seaman, of the murdered steward.

His mother was there now to comfort him.

"I haven't been to bed, dear. I couldn't leave you like that. I've been waiting and praying for you. You're ready to come now, aren't you?"

"Yes, Mother, I'm ready."

"I love you so. All loving is suffering."

Silence fell. Mr. Pinfold put his weapons away and drew back the shutter. It was dawn. He lay on his bed wide awake, his rage quite abated, calmly considering the events of the night.

There had been no funeral. So much seemed certain. Indeed the whole incident of Captain Steerforth and Goneril and the murdered steward had become insubstantial under the impact of the new assault. Mr. Pinfold's orderly, questing mind began to sift the huge volume of charges which had been made against him. Some — that he was Jewish and homosexual, that he had stolen a moonstone and left his mother to die a pauper — were totally preposterous. Others were inconsistent. If, for example, he were a newly arrived immigrant, he could not have been a rowdy undergraduate at Oxford; if he were so anxious to establish himself as a countryman, he would not have slighted his neighbours. The young

105

men in their drunken rage had clearly roared out any abuse that came to mind, but there emerged from the chaotic uproar the basic facts that he was generally disliked on board the *Caliban,* that two at least of his fellow-passengers were possessed by fanatical hate, and that they had some sort of indirect personal acquaintance with him. How else could they have heard, even in its wildly garbled form, of his wife's transactions with Hill (who was well and prosperous when Mr. Pinfold last heard of him)? They came from his part of the country. It was not unlikely that Hill, while boasting of his astuteness among his cronies, had told a story of oppression elsewhere. If that was the sort of thing that was being said in the district, Mr. Pinfold should correct it. Mr. Pinfold had to consider also his comfort during the coming voyage. He required peace of mind in which to work. These dreadful young men were likely, whenever they got drunk, to come caterwauling outside his cabin. On a later occasion, moreover, they might attempt physical assault, might even succeed in it. The result could only be humiliating; it might be painful. The world teemed with journalists. He imagined his wife reading in her morning paper a cable from Aden or Port

Soudan describing the fracas. Something must be done. He could lay the matter before the Captain, the natural guardian of law in his ship, but with this thought there emerged again from oblivion the matter of the Captain's own culpability. Mr. Pinfold was going to have the Captain arrested for murder at the earliest opportunity. Nothing would suit that black heart better than to have the only witness against him involved in a brawl — or silenced in one. A new suspicion took shape. Mr. Pinfold had been indiscreet at dinner in revealing his private knowledge. Was it not probable that Captain Steerforth had instigated the whole attack? Where had the young men been drinking after the bar was shut, if not in the Captain's cabin?

Mr. Pinfold began to shave. This prosaic operation recalled him to strict reason. The Captain's guilt was not proven. First things first. He must deal with the young men. He studied the passenger list. There was no Fosker on it. Mr. Pinfold himself, when crossing the Atlantic, avoided interviewers by remaining incognito. It seemed unlikely that Fosker would have the same motive. Perhaps the police were after him. The other man was ostensibly respectable; four of a name should be easy to find.

But there seemed to be no family of father, mother, son and daughter in that list. Mr. Pinfold lathered his face for the second shave. He was puzzled. It was unlikely that so large a party would join the ship at the last moment, after the list had been printed. They did not sound the kind of people given to impetuous dashes abroad — and, anyway such people travelled by air nowadays. And there was that other General travelling with them. Mr. Pinfold gazed at his puzzled, soapy face. Then he saw light. Stepfather, that was it. He and the mother would bear one name, the children another. Mr. Pinfold would keep his eyes and ears open. It should not be difficult to identify them.

Mr. Pinfold dressed carefully. He chose a Brigade tie to wear that morning and a cap that matched his tweed suit. He went on deck, where seamen were at work swabbing. They had already cleaned up all traces of the night's disgusting climax. He ascended to the main, promenade deck. It was a morning such as at any other time would have elated him. Even now, with so much to harass him, he was conscious of exhilaration. He stood alone, breathing deeply, making light of his annoyances.

Margaret, somewhere quite near, said: "Look, he's

left his cabin. Doesn't he look smart today? Now's our chance to give him our presents. It's much better than giving them to his steward as we meant to. Now we can arrange them ourselves."

"D'you think he'll like them?" said the other girl.

"He ought to. We've taken enough trouble. They're the best we could possibly get."

"But, Meg, he's so *grand.*"

"It's because he's grand he'll like them. Grand people are always pleased with *little* things. He *must* have his presents this morning. After the silly way the boys behaved last night it will show him *we* weren't in it. At least not in it in the way they were. He'll see that as far as we're concerned it was all fun and love."

"Suppose he comes in and finds us?"

"You keep *cave.* If he starts going down, sing."

" 'When first I saw Mabel'?"

"Of course. Our song."

Mr. Pinfold was tempted to trap Margaret. He relished the simple male pleasure, rather rare to him in recent years, of being found attractive, and was curious to see this honey-tongued girl. But she inevitably would lead him to the brother and to Fosker, and he was constrained by honour. These presents, whatever they were, constituted a flag of truce. He could not snatch advantage from the girls' generosity.

Presently Margaret rejoined her friend.

"He hasn't moved."

"No, he's just stood there all the time. What do you suppose he's thinking about?"

"Those beastly boys, I expect."

"Do you think he's very upset?"

"He's so brave."

"Often brave people are the most sensitive."

"Well, it will be all right when he gets back to his cabin and finds our presents."

Mr. Pinfold walked the decks for an hour. No passengers were about.

As the gong sounded for breakfast, Mr. Pinfold went below. He stopped first at his cabin to see what Margaret had left for him. All he found was the cup of tea, cold now, which the steward had put there. The bed was made. The place was squared up and ship-shape. There were no presents.

As he left, he met the cabin steward.

"I say, did a young lady leave anything for me in my cabin?"

110

"Yes, sir, breakfast now, sir."

"No. Listen. I think something was left for me here about an hour ago."

"Yes, sir, gong for breakfast just now."

"Oh," said Margaret, "he hasn't found it."

"He must *look.*"

"*Look* for it, Gilbert, *look.*"

He searched the little wardrobe. He peered under the bunk. He opened the cupboard over the wash-hand-basin. There was nothing there.

"There's nothing there," said Margaret. "He can't find it. He can't find anything," she said on a soft note of despair. "The sweet brave idiot, he can't find anything."

So he went down alone to breakfast.

He was the first of the passengers to appear. Mr. Pinfold was hungry. He ordered coffee and fish and eggs and fruit. He was about to eat when ping! the little, rose-shaded electric lamp which stood on the table before him came into action as a transmitter. The delinquent youths were awake and up and on the air again, their vitality unimpaired by the excesses of the night.

"Haloo-loo-loo-loo-loo. Hark-ark-ark-ark-ark," they holloaed. "Loo in there. Fetch him out. Yoicks."

"I fear Fosker is not entirely conversant with sporting parlance," said the General.

"Hark-ark-ark-ark. Come out, Peinfeld. We know where you are. We've got you." A whip-crack. "Ow," from Fosker, "look out what you're doing with that hunting crop."

"Run, Peinfeld, run. We can see you. We're coming for you."

The steward at that moment was at Mr. Pinfold's side serving him with haddock. He seemed unconscious of the cries emanating from the lamp; to him presumably they were all one with the unreasonable variety of knives and forks and the superfluity of inedible foods; all part of the complexity of this remote and rather disgusting Western way of life.

Mr. Pinfold ate stolidly. The young men resumed the diatribe, repeating again in clear, morning voices the garbled accusations of the night before. Interspersed with them was the challenge: "Come and meet us, Gilbert. You're afraid, Peinfeld. We want to talk to you, Peinfeld. You're hiding, aren't you? You're afraid to come and talk."

Margaret spoke: "Oh, Gilbert, what are they doing to you? Where are you? You musn't let them find you. Come to me. I'll hide you. You never found

112

your presents and now they are after you again. Let
me look after you, Gilbert. It's me, Mimi. Don't you
trust me?"

Mr. Pinfold turned to his scrambled eggs. He had
forgotten, when he ordered them, that they would
not be fresh. Now he beckoned to the steward to re-
move them.

"Off your feed, Gilbert? You're in a funk, aren't
you? Can't eat when you're in a funk, can you? Poor
Gilbert, too scared to eat." They began to give instructions for a place of meeting. ". . . D. Deck, turn
right, Got that! You'll see some lockers. The next
bulkhead. We're waiting for you. Better come now
and get it over. You've got to meet us some time,
you know. We've got you, Gilbert. We've got you.
There's no escape. Better get it over . . . "

Mr. Pinfold's patience was exhausted. He must
put a stop to this nonsense. Recalling some vague
memories of signal procedure in the army, he drew
the lamp towards him and spoke into it curtly: "Pinfold to hooligans. Rendezvous main lounge 0930
hours. Out."

The lamp was not designed to be moved. His
pull disconnected it in some way. The bulb went
out and the voices abruptly ceased. At the same

113

moment Glover came into breakfast. "Hullo, something gone wrong with the light?"

"I tried to move it. I hope you slept better last night?"

"Like a log. No more disturbances, I hope?"

Mr. Pinfold considered whether or not to confide in Glover and decided immediately, no.

"No," he said, and ordered some cold ham.

The dining-saloon filled. Mr. Pinfold exchanged greetings. He went on deck, keeping alert, hoping to spot his persecutors, thinking it possible that Margaret would make herself known to him. But he saw no hooligans; half a dozen healthy girls passed him, some in trousers and duffle coats, some in tweed skirts and sweaters; one might be Margaret but none gave him a sign. At half past nine he took an arm chair in a corner of the lounge and waited. He had his blackthorn with him; it was just conceivable that the youths were so frenzied that they might attempt violence even here, in the daylight.

He began to rehearse the coming interview. He was the judge. He had summoned these men to appear before him. Something like a regimental orderly room, he thought, would be the proper atmosphere. He was the commanding officer hearing a

114

charge of brawling. His powers of punishment were meagre. He would admonish them severely and threaten them with civil penalities.

He would remind them that they were subject to British law in the *Caliban* just as much as on land; that defamation of character and physical assault were grave crimes which would prejudice their whole future careers. He would "throw the whole book" at them. He would explain icily that he was entirely indifferent to their good or bad opinion; that he regarded their friendship and their enmity as equally impertinent. But he would also hear what they had to say for themselves. A good officer knows the enormous ills that can arise from men brooding on imaginary grudges. These defaulters were clearly suffering from a number of delusions about himself. It was better that they should get it off their chests, hear the truth and then shut up for the rest of the voyage. Moreover if, as seemed certain, these delusions derived from rumours which were in circulation among Mr. Pinfold's neighbours, he must plainly investigate and scotch them.

He had the lounge to himself. The rest of the passengers were ranged along the deck in their chairs and rugs. The unvarying hum of marine

115

mechanical life was the only sound. The clock over the little bandstand read quarter to ten. Mr. Pinfold decided to give them till ten; then he would go to the wireless office and inform his wife of his recovery. It was beneath his dignity to attend on these dreadful young men.

Some similar point of pride seemed to influence them. Above the hum he presently heard them discussing him. The voices came from the panelling near his head. First in his cabin, then in the dining-saloon, now here, the surviving strands of war-time intercommunication were fitfully active. The whole wiring of the ship was in need of a thorough overhaul, Mr. Pinfold thought; for all he knew there might be a danger of fire.

"We'll talk to Peinfeld when it suits us and not a moment before."

"Who'll do the talking?"

"I will, of course."

"Do you know what you're going to say?"

"Of course."

"Not really much point in my coming at all, is there?"

"I may need you as a witness."

"All right, come on then. Let's see him now."

116

"When it suits *me*, Fosker, not before."

"What are we waiting for?"

"To let him get into a thorough funk. Remember at school one was always kept waiting for a beating? Just to make it taste sweeter? Well, Peinfeld can wait for *his* beating."

"He's scared stiff."

"He's practically blubbing now."

At ten o'clock Mr. Pinfold took out his watch, verified the time shown on the clock, and rose from the corner. "He's going away." "He's running away." "Funk," came faintly from the fumed-oak panelling. Mr. Pinfold climbed to the wireless office on the boat deck, composed a message and handed it in: *"Pinfold. Lychpole. Entirely cured. All love. Gilbert."*

"Is that address enough?" asked the clerk.

"Yes. There's only one telegraph office called Lychpole in the country."

He walked the decks, thought his blackthorn superfluous and returned to his cabin, where the B.B.C. was loudly in possession. ". . . in the studio Jimmy Lance, who is well known to all listeners and Miss June Cumberleigh, who is new to listeners. Jimmy is going to let us see what is probably a unique col-

117

lection. He has kept every letter he ever received. That's so, isn't it, Jimmy?"

"Well, not letters from the Income Tax Collector."

"Ha. Ha."

"Ha. Ha."

A great burst of unrestrained laughter from the unseen audience.

"No, none of us like to be reminded of that kind of letter, Jimmy, do we? Ha Ha. But I think in your time you have had letters from a great many celebrities?"

"And from some pretty dim people, too."

"Ha. Ha."

"Ha. Ha. Ha."

"Well, June is going to take letters at random out of your file and read them. Ready, June? Right. The first letter is from — "

Mr. Pinfold knew June Cumberleigh and liked her. She was a wholly respectable, clever, funny-faced girl who had got drawn into bohemia through her friendship with James Lance. It was not her natural voice that she now used. Through some mechanical distortion she spoke in almost identical tones to Goneril's.

"Gilbert Pinfold," she said.

118

"And do you count him among the celebrities or the dim people, Jimmy?"

"A celebrity."

"Do you?" said June. "I think he's a dreadfully dim little man."

"Well, what's the dim little man got to say?"

"It is so badly written I can't read it."

Enormous amusement in the audience.

"Try another."

"Who is it this time?"

"Why. This is *too* much. Gilbert Pinfold again."

"Ha, ha, ha, ha, ha."

Mr. Pinfold left his cabin, slamming the door on this deplorable entertainment. James, he knew, did a lot of broadcasting. He was a poet and artist by nature who had let himself become popularized; but this exhibition was a bit thick, even for him. And what was June doing? She must have lost all sense of decency.

Mr. Pinfold walked the decks. He was still troubled by the unsolved problem of the hooligans. Something would have to be done about them. But he felt reassured about Captain Steerforth. Now that it was apparent that many of the sounds in his cabin emanated from Broadcasting House, he became certain that what he had overheard was part of a play. The similarity of June's voice and Goneril's seemed to confirm it. He had been an ass to suppose Captain Steerforth a murderer; it was part of the confusion of mind caused by Dr. Drake's pills. And if Captain Steerforth were innocent, then he was a potential, a natural ally against his enemies.

Thus comforted, Mr. Pinfold returned to his listening post in the corner of the lounge. Father and son were in conference.

"Fosker's wet."

"Yes. I've never thought anything of him."

"I'm leaving him out of this business from now on."

"Very wise. But you've got to go through with it yourself, you know. You didn't come very creditably out of last night's affair. I've no great objection to your knocking the fellow about a bit if he deserves it. Anway you've threatened him and you've got to do something about it. You can't just drop the matter at this stage. But you want to go about it in the right way. You're up against something rather more dangerous than you realize."

"Dangerous? That cowardly, common little communist pansy —"

120

"Yes, yes. I know how you feel. But I've seen a bit more of the world than you have, my boy. I think I'd better put you up to a few wrinkles. In the first place Pinfold is utterly unscrupulous. He has no gentlemanly instincts. He's quite capable of taking you to the courts. Have you any proof of your charges?"

"Everyone knows they're true."

"That may be but it won't mean a thing in a court of law unless you can prove it. You need evidence so strong that Pinfold daren't sue you. And, so far, you haven't got it. Another thing, Pinfold is enormously rich. I daresay for example he owns a controlling share in this shipping line. Pinfold has money salted away in half a dozen countries. He has friends everywhere."

"*Friends?*"

"Well, no, not friends as *we* understand them. But he has influence — with politicians, with the police. You've lived in a small world, my boy. You have no conception of the ramifications of power of a man like Pinfold in the modern age. He's attractive to women — homosexuals always are. Margaret is distinctly taken with him. Even your mother doesn't really dislike him. We've got to work cautiously and build up a party against him. I'll send off a few radio-

121

grams. There are one or two people I know who, I think, may be able to give us some *facts* about Pinfold. It's facts we need. We've got to make out an absolutely water-tight case. Till then, lie low."

"You don't think I ought to beat him up?"

"Well, I wouldn't go so far as to say that. If you find him alone, you might have a smack at him. I know what I should have done myself at your age. But I'm old now and wise and my advice is lie low, work under cover. Then in a day or two we may have something to surprise our celebrated fellow passenger . . . "

When noon was sounded Mr. Pinfold went aft and ordered himself a cocktail. There was the usual jollity over the sweepstake. He looked at the flag on the chart. The *Caliban* had rounded Cape St. Vincent and was well on the way to Gibraltar. She should pass the straits that night into the Mediterranean. When he went down to luncheon he was in a hopeful mood. The hooligans had fallen out and their rage had been tempered. The Mediterranean had always welcomed Mr. Pinfold in the past. His annoyance would be over, he believed, once he was in those hallowed waters.

In the dining-saloon he noticed that the dark man who had sat alone was now at a table with Mrs. Cockson and Mrs. Benson. In a curious way that too seemed a good omen.

The
International
Incident

I T WAS the conversation of the two Generals, overheard as he lay in his cabin after luncheon, which
first made Mr. Pinfold aware of the international
crisis which had been developing while he lay ill.
There had been no hint of it in the newspapers he
had listlessly scanned before embarkation; or, if
there had been, he had not, in this confused state,
appreciated its importance. Now, it appeared, there
was a first class row about the possession of Gibraltar. Some days ago the Spaniards had laid formal,
peremptory claim to the fortress and were now exer-
cising the very dubious right of stopping and search-
ing ships passing through the straits in what they
defined as their territorial waters. During luncheon
the *Caliban* had hove-to and Spanish officials had

come on board. They were demanding that the ship put into Algeciras for an examination of cargo and passengers.

The two Generals were incensed against General Franco and made free use of "tin-pot dictator," "two-penny-halfpenny Hitler," "priest-ridden puppet" and similar opprobrious epithets. They also spoke contemptuously of the British government who were prepared to "truckle" to him.

"It's nothing short of a blockade. If I were in command I'd call their bluff, go full steam ahead and tell them to shoot and be damned."

"That would be an act of war, of course."

"Serve 'em right. We haven't sunk so low that we can't lick the Spaniards, I hope."

"It's all this UNO."

"And the Americans."

"Anyway, this is one thing that can't be blamed on Russia."

"It means the end of NATO."

"Good riddance."

"The Captain has to take his orders from home, I suppose."

"That's the trouble. He can't get any orders."

Captain Steerforth was now fully restored to Mr.

Pinfold's confidence. He saw him as a simple sailor obliged to make a momentous decision, not only for the safety of his own vessel but for the peace of the world. Throughout that long afternoon Mr. Pinfold followed the frantic attempts of the signalmen to get into touch with the shipping company, the Foreign Office, the Governor of Gibraltar, the Mediterranean fleet. All were without avail. Captain Steerforth stood quite alone as the representative of international justice and British prestige. Mr. Pinfold thought of Jenkin's ear and the Private of the Buffs. Captain Steerforth was a good man forced into an importance quite beyond his capabilities. Mr. Pinfold wished he could stand beside him on the bridge, exhort him to defiance, run the ship under the Spanish guns into the wide, free inland sea where all the antique heroes of history and legend had sailed to glory.

As factions resolve in common danger, Mr. Pinfold forgot the enmity of the young hooligans. All on board the *Caliban* were comrades-in-arms against foreign aggression.

The Spanish officials were polite enough. Mr. Pinfold could hear them talking in the Captain's cabin. In excellent English they explained how deeply re-

126

pugnant they, personally, found the orders they had to carry out. It was a question of politics, they said. No doubt the matter would be adjusted satisfactorily at a congress. Meanwhile they could only obey. They spoke of some enormous indemnity which, if it were forthcoming from London, would immediately ensure the *Caliban's* free passage. A time was mentioned, midnight, after which if no satisfactory arrangements were made, the *Caliban* would be taken under escort to Algeciras.

"Piracy," said Captain Steerforth." "Blackmail."

"We cannot allow such language about the Head of the State."

"Then you can bloody well get off my bridge," said the Captain. They withdrew but nothing was settled by the tiff. They remained on board and the ship lay motionless.

Towards evening Mr. Pinfold went on deck. There was no sign of land, nor of the Spanish ship which had brought the officials and, presumably, was lying off somewhere below the horizon. Mr. Pinfold leaned over the rail and looked down at the flowing sea. The sun was dead astern of them sinking low over the water. Had he not known better, he would have supposed they were still steaming forward, so swiftly and steadily ran the current. He recalled that he had once been taught that through the Suez Canal the Indian Ocean emptied itself into the Atlantic. He thought of the multitudinous waters that supplied the Mediterranean, the ice-flows of the Black Sea that raced past Constantinople and Troy; the great rivers of history, the Nile, the Euphrates, the Danube, the Rhone. They it was that broke across the bows and left a foaming wake.

The passengers seemed quite unaware of the doom which threatened the ship. Fresh from their siestas they sat about that afternoon just as they had sat before, reading and talking and knitting. There was the same little group on the sports deck. Mr. Pinfold met Glover.

"Did you see the Spaniards come on board?" he asked.

"Spaniards? Come on board? How could they? When?"

"They're causing a lot of trouble."

"I'm awfully sorry," said Glover. "I simply don't know what you're talking about."

"You will," said Mr. Pinfold. "Soon enough, I fear."

Glover looked at him with the keen, perplexed

air which he often assumed now when Mr. Pinfold spoke to him.

"There aren't any Spaniards on board that I know of."

It was not Mr. Pinfold's duty to spread alarm and despondency or explain his unique sources of information. The Captain plainly wanted the secret kept as long as possible.

"I daresay I'm mistaken," said Mr. Pinfold loyally.

"There are the Burmese and the Norwegian couple at our table. They're the only foreigners I've seen."

"Yes. A misunderstanding, no doubt."

Glover went to the space in the bows where he swung his club. He swung it methodically, with concentration, without a thought of Spaniards.

Mr. Pinfold withdrew to his listening post in the corner of the lounge but nothing was to be heard there except the tapping of Morse as the signalmen sent out their calls for help. One of them said: "Nothing coming in at all. I don't believe our signals are going out."

"It's that new device," said his mate. "I heard something had been invented to create wireless silence. It's not been tried before, as far as I know.

It was developed too late to use in the war. Both sides were at work on it but it was still in the experimental stage in nineteen forty-five."

"More effective than jamming."

"Different principle altogether. They can only do it at short range so far. In a year or two it'll develop so that they can isolate whole countries."

"Where will our jobs be then?"

"Oh, someone'll find a counter-system. They always do."

"Anyway all we can do now is keep on trying."

The tapping recommenced. Mr. Pinfold went to the bar and ordered himself a glass of gin and bitters. The English steward came in from the deck, tray in hand, and went to the serving hatch.

"Those Spanish bastards are asking for whisky," he said.

"I'll not serve them," said the man who handled the bottles.

"Captain's orders," said the steward.

"What's come over the old man? It isn't like him to take a thing like this lying down."

"He's got a plan. Trust him. Now give me those four whiskies and I hope it poisons them."

Mr. Pinfold finished his drink and returned to his

listening post. He was curious to know more of the Captain's plan. He had so sooner settled in his chair and attuned his ear to the panelling than he heard the Captain; he was in his cabin addressing the officers.

" . . . all question of international law and convention apart" he was saying, "there is a particular reason why we cannot allow this ship to be searched. You all know we have an extra man on board. He's not a passenger. He's not one of the crew. He doesn't appear on any list. He's got no ticket or papers. I don't even know his name myself. I daresay you've noticed him sitting alone in the dining-saloon. All I've been told is that he's very important indeed to HMG. He's on a special mission. That's why he's travelling with us instead of on one of the routes that are watched. It's him, of course, that the Spaniards are after. All this talk about territorial waters and right of search is pure bluff. We've got to see that that man gets through."

"How are you going to manage that, Skipper?"

"I don't know yet. But I've got an idea. I think I shall have to take the passengers into my confidence — not all of them, of course, and not fully into my confidence. But I'm going to collect half a dozen

131

of the more responsible men and put them in the picture — into a bit of the picture anyway. I'll ask them up here, casually, after dinner. With their help the plan *may* work."

The Generals received their invitation early and were not deceived by its casual form. They were discussing it while Mr. Pinfold dressed for dinner.

"It looks as though he's decided to put up a fight."

"We'll all stand by him."

"Can we trust those Burmese?"

"That's a question to raise at the meeting to-night."

"Wouldn't trust 'em myself."

"The Norwegians?"

"They seem sound enough but this is a British affair."

"Always happier on our own, eh?"

It did not occur to Mr. Pinfold that he might be omitted from the Captain's *cadre*. But no invitation reached him although in various other parts of the ship he heard confidential messages. "The Captain's compliments and he would be grateful if you could find it convenient to come to his cabin for a few minutes after dinner. . . . "

At table Captain Steerforth carried his anxieties with splendid composure. Mrs. Scarfield actually asked him: "When do we go through the straits?" and he replied without any perceptible nuance: "Early tomorrow morning."

"It ought to get warmer then?"

"Not at this time of year," he answered nonchalantly. "You must wait for the Red Sea before you go into whites."

During their brief acquaintance Mr. Pinfold had regarded this man with sharply varying emotions. Unquestionable admiration filled him when, at the end of dinner, Mrs. Scarfield asked: "Are you joining us for a rubber?" and he replied: "Not this evening, I'm afraid. I've one or two things to see to," but though Mr. Pinfold hung back so that he left the dining-saloon at the Captain's side, giving him the chance to invite him to the conference, they parted at the head of the stair without the word being said. Rather nonplussed, Mr. Pinfold hesitated, then decided to go to his cabin. It was essential that he should be easily found when he was wanted.

Soon it was apparent that he was not wanted at

133

all. Captain Steerforth had his party promptly assembled and he began by giving them a résumé of the situation as Mr. Pinfold already understood it. He said nothing of the secret agent. He merely explained that he had been unable to obtain authorization from his company to pay the preposterous sum demanded. The alternative offered by the Spaniards was that he should put into Algeciras until the matter had been settled between Madrid and London. That, he said, would be a betrayal of every standard of British seamanship. The *Caliban* would not strike her flag. There was a burst of restrained, husky, emotional, male applause. He explained his plan: at midnight the Spanish ship would come alongside. The officials now on board would tranship to her to report the results of their demand. They intended to take with them under arrest himself and a party of hostages and to put an officer of their own on his bridge to sail her into the Spanish port. It was in the dark, on the gangway, that the resistance would disclose itself. The English would overpower the Spaniards, throw them back into their ship — "and if one or two go into the drink in the process, so much the better" — and the *Caliban* would then make full steam ahead. "I don't think when it comes

134

to the point, they'll open fire. Anyway their gunnery is pretty moderate and I consider it's a risk we have to take. You are all agreed?"

"Agreed." "Agreed." "Agreed."

"I knew I could trust you," said the Captain. "You're all men who've seen service. I am proud to have you under my command. The Burmese will be locked in their cabins."

"How about Pinfold?" asked one of the Generals. "Shouldn't he be here?"

"There is a role assigned to Captain Pinfold. I don't think I need go into that at the moment."

"Has he received his orders?"

"Not yet," said Captain Steerforth. "We have some hours before us. I suggest, gentlemen, that you go about the ship in the normal way, turn in early, and rendezvous here at eleven forty-five. Midnight is zero hour. Perhaps, General, you will remain behind for a few minutes. For the present, good night, gentlemen."

The meeting broke up. Presently only the General remained with the first and second officers in the Captain's cabin.

"Well," said Captain Steerforth, "how did that sound?"

"Pretty thin, Skipper, if you ask me," said the first officer.

"I take it," said the General, "that what we have just heard was merely the cover-plan?"

"Precisely. I could hardly hope to deceive an old campaigner like you. I am sorry not to be able to take your companions into my confidence, but in the interest of security I have had to limit those in the know to an absolute minimum. The role of the committee who have just left us is to create sufficient diversion to enable us to carry out the real purpose of the operation. That, of course, is to prevent a certain person falling into the hands of the enemy."

"Pinfold?"

"No, no, quite the contrary. Captain Pinfold, I fear, has to be written off. The Spaniards will not let us pass until they think they have their man. It has not been an easy decision, I assure you. I am responsible for the safety of all my passengers, but at a time like this sacrifices have to be accepted. The plan briefly is this. Captain Pinfold is to impersonate the agent. He will be provided with papers identifying him. The Spaniards will take him ashore and the ship will sail on unmolested."

There was a pause while this proposition was considered. The first officer at length spoke. "It might work, Skipper."

"It *must* work."

"What do you suppose will happen to him?"

"Can't say. I suppose they'll hold him under arrest while they investigate. They won't let him communicate with our embassy, of course. When they find out their mistake, if they ever do, they'll be in rather a jam. They may let him out or they may find it more convenient just to let him disappear."

"I see."

It was the General who voiced the thought uppermost in Mr. Pinfold's mind. "Why Pinfold?" he asked.

"It was a painful choice," said Captain Steerforth, "but not a difficult one. He is the obvious man, really. No one else on board would take them in for a moment. He looks like a secret agent. I think he was one during the war. He's a sick man and therefore expendable. And, of course, he's a Roman Catholic. That ought to make things a little easier for him in Spain."

"Yes," said the General, "yes. I see all that. But all

137

the same I think it's pretty sporting of him to agree. In his place I must own I'd think twice before taking it on."

"Oh, *he* doesn't know anything about it."

"The devil he doesn't?"

"No, that would be quite fatal to security. Besides he might *not* agree. He has a wife, you know, and a large family. You can't really blame a man who thinks of domestic responsibilities before volunteering for hazardous service. No, Captain Pinfold must be kept quite in the dark. That's the reason for the counter-plan, the diversion. There's got to be a schemozzle on the gangway so that Captain Pinfold can be pushed into the corvette. You, number one, will be responsible for hauling him out of his cabin and planting the papers on him."

"Aye, aye, sir."

"That boy of mine will laugh," said the General. "He took against Pinfold from the start. Now he hears he's deserted to the enemy. . . . "

The voices ceased. For a long time Mr. Pinfold sat paralyzed with horror and rage. When at length he looked at his watch he found that it was nearly half past nine. Then he took off his evening clothes and put on his tweeds. Whatever outrage the night

138

brought forth should find him suitably dressed. He pocketed his passport and his travellers' cheques. Then, blackthorn in hand, he sat down again and began patiently and painfully, as he had learned in the army, to "appreciate the situation." He was alone without hope of reinforcement. His sole advantage was that he knew, and they did not know he knew, their plan of action. He examined the Captain's plan in the light of the quite considerable experience he had acquired in small-scale night operations and he found it derisory. The result of a scuffle in the dark on a gangway was quite unpredictable but he was confident that, forewarned, he could easily evade or repulse any attempt to put him into the corvette against his will. Even if they succeeded and the *Caliban* attempted to sail away the corvette, of course, would open fire and, of course, would sink or disable her long before the Spaniards began examining the forged papers that were to be planted on him.

And here Mr. Pinfold experienced scruples. He was not what is generally meant by the appellation a "philanthropic" man; he totally lacked what was now called a "social conscience." But apart from his love of family and friends he had a certain basic

139

kindliness to those who refrained from active annoyance. And in an old-fashioned way he was patriotic. These sentiments sometimes did service for what are generally regarded as the higher loyalties and affections. This was such an occasion. He rather liked Mrs. Scarfield, Mrs. Cockson, Mrs. Benson, Glover and all those simple, chatting, knitting, dozing passengers. For the unseen, enigmatic Margaret he felt tender curiosity. It would be a pity for all these to be precipitated into a watery bier by the ineptitude of Captain Steerforth. For himself he had little concern but he knew that his disappearance, and possible disgrace, would grieve his wife and family. It was intolerable that this booby Captain should handle so many lives so clumsily. But there was also the question of the secret agent. If this man, as seemed likely, was really of vital importance to his country, he must be protected. Mr. Pinfold felt responsible for his protection. He had been chosen as victim. That doom was inescapable. But he would go to the sacrifice a garlanded hero. He would not be tricked into it.

No precise tactical plan could be made. Whatever his action, it would be improvised. But the intention was plain. He would, if necessary, consent to impersonate the agent but Captain Steerforth and his cronies must understand that he went voluntarily as a man of honour and Mrs. Pinfold must be fully informed of the circumstances. That established, he would consent to his arrest.

As he pondered all this, he was barely conscious of the voices that came to him. He waited.

At a quarter to twelve there was a hail from the bridge answered from the sea in Spanish. The corvette was coming alongside and at once the ship came to life with a multitude of voices. This, Mr. Pinfold decided, was his moment to act. He must deliver his terms to the Captain before the Spaniards came on board. Gripping his blackthorn, he left the cabin.

Immediately his communications were cut. The lighted corridor was empty and completely silent. He strode down it to the stairway, mounted to the main deck. No one was about. There was no ship near or anywhere in sight; not a light anywhere on the dark horizon; not a sound from the bridge; only the rush and slap of the waves along the ship's side, and the keen sea wind. Mr. Pinfold stood confounded, the only troubled thing in a world at peace.

He had been dauntless a minute before in the

face of his enemies. Now he was struck with real fear, something totally different from the superficial alarms he had once or twice known in moments of danger, something he had quite often read about and dismissed as over-writing. He was possessed from outside himself with atavistic panic. "Oh, let me not be mad, not mad, sweet heaven," he cried.

And in that moment of agony there broke not far from him in the darkness peal upon rising peal of mocking laughter — Goneril's. It was not an emollient sound. It was devoid of mirth, an obscene cacophony of pure hatred. But it fell on Mr. Pinfold's ears at that moment like a nursery lullaby.

"A hoax," he said to himself.

It was all a hoax on the part of the hooligans. He understood all. They had learned the secret of the defective wiring in his cabin. Somehow they had devised a means of controlling it, somehow they had staged this whole charade to tease him. It was spiteful and offensive, no doubt; it must not happen again. But Mr. Pinfold felt nothing but gratitude in his discovery. He might be unpopular; he might be ridiculous; but he was not mad.

He returned to his cabin. He had been awake now for thirty or forty hours. He lay down and at once in his clothes and fell into deep, natural sleep. He lay motionless and unconscious for six hours.

When he next went on deck the sun was up, directly over the bows. Square on the port beam rose the unmistakable peak of the Rock. The *Caliban* was steaming into the calm Mediterranean.

◄6►

The Human Touch

WHILE MR. PINFOLD was shaving, he heard
Margaret say: "It was an absolutely beastly
joke and I'm glad it fell flat."

"It came off very nicely," said her brother. "Old
Peinfeld was jibbering with funk."

"He wasn't — and he isn't called Peinfeld. He was
a hero. When I saw him standing there alone on
deck I thought of Nelson."

"He was drunk."

"He says it's not drink, dear," said their mother,
gently uncommitted to either side. "He *says* it's some
medicine he has to take."

"Medicine from a brandy bottle."

"I know you're wrong," said Margaret. "You see

it just happens *I know* what he's thinking, and you don't."

Then Goneril's steely voice cut in: "*I* can tell you what he was doing on deck. He was screwing up his courage to jump overboard. He longs to kill himself, don't you, Gilbert. All right, I know you're listening down there. You can hear me, can't you, Gilbert? You wish you were dead, don't you, Gilbert. And a very good idea, too. Why don't you do it, Gilbert? Why not? Perfectly easy. It would save us all — you too, Gilbert — a great deal of trouble."

"Beast," said Margaret and broke into weeping.

"Oh God," said her brother, "now you've turned on the water-works again."

Mr. Pinfold was fortified by his six hours' sleep. He went above, leaving the nagging voices of the cabin for the silent and empty decks for an hour. The Rock had dropped below the horizon and there was no land in sight. The sea might have been any sea by the look of it, but he knew it was the Mediterranean, that splendid enclosure which held all the world's history and half the happiest memories of his own life; of work and rest and battle, of aesthetic adventure and of young love.

145

After breakfast he took a book to the lounge, not to his listening-post in the panelled corner but to an isolated chair in the centre, and read undisturbed. He must get out of that haunted cabin, he thought; but not yet; later, in his own time.

Presently he rose and began once more to walk the decks. They were thronged now. All the passengers seemed to be there, occupied as before in reading, knitting, dozing or strolling like himself, but that morning he found a kind of paschal novelty in the scene and rejoiced in it until he was rudely disturbed in his benevolence.

The passengers too seemed aware of change. They must all at one time or another in the last few days have caught sight of Mr. Pinfold. Now, however, it was as though he were a noteworthy, unaccompanied female, newly appearing in the evening promenade of some stagnant South American town. He had been witness of such an event on many a dusty plaza; he had seen the sickly faces of the men brighten, their lassitude take sudden life; he had observed the little flourishes of seedy dandyism; he had heard the jungle whistles and, without fully understanding them, the frank, anatomical appraisals; had seen the sly following and pinching of the

146

unwary tourist. In just that way Mr. Pinfold, where-ever he went that day, found himself to be such a cynosure; everyone was talking about him, loudly and unashamedly, but not in his praise.

"That's Gilbert Pinfold, the writer."

"That common little man? It can't be."

"Have you read his books? He has a very *peculiar* sense of humour, you know."

"He is very peculiar altogether. His hair is very long."

"He's wearing lip-stick."

"He's painted up to the eyes."

"But he's so shabby. I thought people like that were always smart."

"There are different types of homosexual, you know. What are called 'poufs' and 'nancies' — that is the dressy kind. Then there are the others they call 'butch.' I read a book about it. Pinfold is a 'butch.'"

That was the first conversation Mr. Pinfold over-heard. He stopped, turned and tried to stare out of countenance the little group of middle-aged women who were speaking. One of them smiled at him and then turning, said: "I believe he's trying to get to know us."

"How disgusting."

Mr. Pinfold walked on but wherever he went he was the topic.

" . . . Lord of the Manor of Lychpole."

"Anyone can be that. It's often a title that goes with some tumble-down farmhouse these days."

"Oh, Pinfold lives in great style I can tell you. Footmen in livery."

"I can guess what he does with the footmen."

"Not any more. He's been impotent for years, you know. That's why he's always thinking of death."

"Is he always thinking of death?"

"Yes. He'll commit suicide one of these days, you'll see."

"I thought he was a Catholic. They aren't allowed to commit suicide, are they?"

"That wouldn't stop Pinfold. He doesn't really *believe* in his religion, you know. He just pretends to because he thinks it aristocratic. It goes with being Lord of the Manor."

"There's only one Lychpole in the world, he told the wireless man."

"Only one Lychpole and Pinfold is its Lord . . ."

" . . . There he is, drunk again."

"He looks ghastly."

148

"A dying man, if ever I saw one."

"Why doesn't he kill himself?"

"Give him time. He's doing his best. Drink and drugs. He daren't go to a doctor, of course, for fear he'd be put in a home."

"Best place for him, I should have thought."

"Best place for him would be over the side."

"Rather a nuisance for poor Captain Steerforth."

"It's a great nuisance for Captain Steerforth having him on board."

"And at his own table."

"That's being taken care of. Haven't you heard? There's going to be a petition."

" . . . Yes, I've signed. Everyone has, I believe."

"Except those actually at the table. The Scarfields wouldn't, or Glover."

"I see it might be a little awkward for them."

"It's a very well-worded petition."

"Yes. The General did that. It makes no specific accusation, you see, that might be libellous. Simply: *'We the undersigned, for reasons which we are prepared to state in confidence, consider it to be an insult to us, as passengers in the* Caliban, *that Mr. Gilbert Pinfold should sit at the Captain's table, a position of honour for which he is notoriously unsuitable.'* That's very neatly put."

" . . . the Captain ought to lock him up. He has full authority."

"But he hasn't actually *done* anything yet, on board."

This was a pair of genial business-men with whom and the Scarfields Mr. Pinfold had spent half an hour one evening.

"For his own protection. It was a very near thing the other night that those boys didn't beat him up."

"They were drunk."

"They may get drunk again. It would be most unpleasant for everyone if there was a police court case."

"Couldn't something be put in our petition about that?"

"It was discussed. The Generals thought it could best be left to the interview. The Captain is bound to ask them to give their reasons."

"Not in writing."

"Exactly. They don't suggest putting him in the cell. Simply confining him to his cabin."

"He probably has certain legal rights, having paid his fare, to his cabin and his meals."

"But *not* to his meals at the Captain's table."

"There you have the crux."

" . . . No," the Norwegian was saying, "I did not sign anything. It is a British matter. All I know is that he is a fascist. I have heard him speak ill of democracy. We had a few such men in the time of Quisling. We knew what to do with them. But I will not mix in these British affairs."

"I've got a photograph of him in a black shirt taken at one of those Albert Hall meetings before the war."

"That might be useful."

"He was up to his eyes in it. He'd have been locked up under 18 B but he escaped by joining the army."

"He did pretty badly there, I suppose?"

"*Very* badly. There was a scandal in Cairo that had to be hushed up when his Brigade-Major shot himself."

"Blackmail?"

"The next best thing."

"I see he's wearing the Guards tie."

"He wears any kind of tie — old Etonian usually."

151

"*Was* he ever at Eton?"

"He says he was," said Glover.

"Don't you believe it. Board school through and through."

"Or at Oxford?"

"No, no. His whole account of his early life is a lie. No one had ever heard of him until a year or two ago. He's one of a lot of nasty people who crept into prominence during the war. . . . "

" . . . I don't say he's an actual card-carrying member of the Communist party, but he's certainly mixed up with them."

"Most Jews are."

"Exactly. And those 'missing diplomats.' They were friends of his."

"He doesn't know enough to make it worth the Russians' while to take him to Moscow."

"Even the Russians wouldn't want Pinfold."

The most curious encounter of that morning was with Mrs. Cockson and Mrs. Benson. They were sitting as usual on the verandah of the deck-bar, each with her glass, and they were talking French with what seemed to Mr. Pinfold, who spoke the language

152

clumsily, pure accent and idiom. Mrs. Cockson said:
*"Ce Monsieur Pinfold essaie toujours de péné-
trer chez moi, et il a essayé de se faire présenter
à moi plusiers de mes amis. Naturellement j'ai re-
fusé."*

*"Connaissez-vous un seul de ses amis? Il me sem-
ble qu'il a des relations très ordinaires."*

*"On peut toujours se tromper dans le premier
temps sur une relation étrangère. On a fini par s'aper-
cevoir à Paris qu'il n'est pas de notre société . . ."*

It was a put-up job, Mr. Pinfold decided. People
did not normally behave in this way.

When Mr. Pinfold first joined Bellamy's there was
an old earl who sat alone all day and every day in
the corner of the stairs wearing an odd, hard hat and
talking loudly to himself. He had one theme, the
passing procession of his fellow members. Sometimes
he dozed, but in his long waking hours he maintained a running commentary — "That fellow's chin
is too big; dreadful-looking fellow? Never saw
him before. Who let him in? . . . Pick your feet up,
you. Wearing the carpets out. . . . Dreadfully fat
young Crambo's getting. Don't eat, don't drink, it's
just he's hard up. Nothing fattens a man like getting

153

hard up. . . . Poor old Nailsworth, his mother was a whore, so's his wife. They say his daughter's going the same way. . . ." and so on.

In the broad tolerance of Bellamy's this eccentric had been accepted quite fondly. He was dead many years now. It was not conceivable, Mr. Pinfold thought, that all the passengers in the *Caliban* should suddenly have become similarly afflicted. This chatter was designed to be overheard. It was a put-up job. It was in fact the Generals' subtle plan, substituted for the adolescent violence of their young.

Twenty-five years ago or more Mr. Pinfold, who was in love with one of them, used to frequent a house full of bright, cruel girls who spoke their own thieves' slang and played their own games. One of these games was a trick from the schoolroom polished for drawing-room use.

When a stranger came among them, they would all — if the mood took them — put out their tongues at him or her; all, that is to say, except those in his immediate line of sight. As he turned his head, one group of tongues popped in, another popped out. Those girls were adept in dialogue. They had rigid self-control. They never giggled. Those who spoke to the stranger assumed an unnatural sweetness. The aim was to make him catch another with her tongue out. It was a comic performance — the turning head, the flickering, crimson stabs, the tender smiles turning to sudden grimaces, the artificiality of the conversation which soon engendered an unidentifiable discomfort in the most insensitive visitor, made him feel that somehow he was making a fool of himself, made him look at his trouser buttons, at his face in the glass to see whether there was something ridiculous in his appearance.

Some sort of game as this, enormously coarsened, must, Mr. Pinfold supposed, have been devised by the passengers in the *Caliban* for their amusement and his discomfort. Well, he was not going to give them the satisfaction of taking notice of it. He no longer glanced to see who was speaking.

" . . . His mother sold her few little pieces of jewellery, you know, to pay his debts . . . "

" . . . Were his books ever any good?"

"Never *good*. His earlier ones weren't quite as bad as his latest. He's written out."

"He's tried every literary trick. He's finished now and he knows it."

"I suppose he's made a lot of money?"

"Not as much as he pretends. And he's spent every penny. His debts are enormous."

"And of course they'll catch him for income-tax soon."

"Oh, yes. He's been putting in false returns for years. They're investigating him now. They don't hurry. They always get their man in the end."

"They'll get Pinfold."

"He'll have to sell Lychpole."

"His children will go to the board school."

"Just as he did himself."

"No more champagne for Pinfold."

"No more cigars."

"I suppose his wife will leave him?"

"Naturally. No home for her. Her family will take her in."

"But not Pinfold."

"No. Not Pinfold . . ."

Mr. Pinfold would not give ground. There must be no appearance of defeat. But in his own time, when he had sauntered long enough, he retired to his cabin.

"Gilbert," said Margaret. "Gilbert. Why don't you

speak to me? You passed quite close to me on deck and you never looked at me. *I* haven't offended you, have I? You know it isn't me who's saying all these beastly things, don't you? Answer me, Gilbert. I can hear you."

So Mr. Pinfold, not uttering the words but pronouncing them in his mind, said: "Where are you? I don't even know you by sight. Why don't we meet, now? Come and have a cocktail with me."

"Oh, Gilbert, darling, you know that's not possible. The *Rules*."

"What rules? Whose? Do you mean your father won't let you?"

"No, Gilbert, not *his* rules, *the* Rules. Don't you understand? It's against *the Rules* for us to meet. I can talk to you now and then but we must never meet."

"What do you look like?"

"I mustn't tell you that. You must find out for yourself. That's one of the Rules."

"You talk as though we were playing some kind of game."

"That's all we are doing — playing a kind of game. I must go now. But there's one thing I'd like to say."

"Well?"

"You won't be offended?"

"I don't expect so."

"Are you sure, darling?"

"What is it?"

"Shall I tell you? Dare I? You won't be offended? Well . . . " Margaret paused and then in a thrilling whisper said: *"Get your hair cut."*

"Well, I'll be damned," said Pinfold; but Margaret was gone and did not hear him.

He looked in the glass. Yes, his hair was rather long. He would get it cut. Then he pondered the new problem: how had Margaret heard his soundless words? That could not be explained on any theory of frayed and crossed wires. As he considered the matter Margaret briefly returned to say: "Not *wires,* darling. *Wireless,*" and then was gone again.

That perhaps should have given him the clue he sought, should have dispelled the mystery that enveloped him. He would learn in good time; at that moment Mr. Pinfold was baffled, almost stupefied, by the occurrences of the morning and he went down to luncheon at the summons of the gong thinking vaguely in terms of telepathy, a subject on which he was ill-informed.

At the table he tackled Glover at once on a question that vexed him. "I was not at Eton," he said suddenly, with a challenge in his voice.

"Nor was I," said Glover. "Marlborough."

"I never said I was at Eton," Mr. Pinfold insisted.

"No. Why should you, I mean, if you weren't?"

"It is a school for which I have every respect, but I was not there myself." Then he turned across to the table to the Norwegian. "I never wore a black shirt in the Albert Hall."

"No?" said the Norwegian, interested but uncomprehending.

"I had every sympathy with Franco during the Civil War."

"Yes? It is so long ago I have rather forgotten what it was all about. In my country we did not pay so much attention as the French and some other nations."

"I never had the smallest sympathy with Hitler."

"No, I suppose not."

"Once I had hopes of Mussolini. But I was never connected with Mosley."

"Mosley? What is that?"

"Please, please," cried pretty Mrs. Scarfield, "don't let's get on to politics."

For the rest of the meal Mr. Pinfold sat silent.

Later he went to the barber's shop and from there to his listening-post in the empty lounge. He saw the ship's surgeon pass the windows. He was on his way, evidently, to the Captain's cabin, for almost immediately Mr. Pinfold heard him say: " . . . I thought I ought to report it to you, Skipper."

"Where was he last seen?"

"In the barber's shop. After that he completely disappeared. He's not in his cabin."

"Why should he have gone overboard?"

"I've had my eye on him ever since we sailed. Haven't you noticed anything odd about him?"

"I've noticed he drinks."

"Yes, he's a typical alcoholic. Several of the passengers asked me to look him over, but I can't, you know, unless he calls me in or unless he does something violent. Now they're all saying he's jumped overboard."

"I'm not going to stop the ship and put out a boat simply because a passenger isn't in his cabin. He's probably in someone else's cabin with one of my female passengers doing you know what."

"Yes, that's the most likely explanation."

"Is there anything the matter with him apart from the bottle?"

"Nothing a day's hard work wouldn't cure. The best thing for him would be to be put swabbing decks for a week. . . ."

And after that the ship, like an aviary, was noisy with calls and chatter.

" . . . He can't be found."

" . . . Overboard."

" . . . No one's seen him since he left the barber . . . "

" . . . The Captain thinks he's got a woman somewhere . . . "

Very wearily Mr. Pinfold tried to shut his mind to these distractions and to read his book. Presently the note changed. "It's all right, he's found."

" . . . False alarm."

" . . . Pinfold's found."

"I'm glad of that," said the General gravely. "I was afraid we might have gone too far."

And the rest was silence.

The cutting of Mr. Pinfold's hair fomented relations with Margaret. She prattled off and on all that afternoon and evening, gloating fondly over the change in Mr. Pinfold's appearance; he looked younger, she said, smarter, altogether more lovable.

Gazing long and earnestly into his looking-glass, turning his head this way and that, Mr. Pinfold saw nothing very different from what he was used to, nothing to justify this enthusiasm. Margaret's gratification, he surmised, sprang less from his enhanced beauty than from the evidence he had given of his trust in her.

Interspersed with her praises there was an occasional hint of some deeper significance: " . . . Think, Gilbert. *Barber's shop.* Doesn't that tell you anything?"

"No. Should it?"

"It's the *clue,* Gilbert. It's what you most want to know, what you *must* know."

"Well, tell me."

"I can't do that, darling. It's against the *Rules.* But I can hint. *Barber's shop,* Gilbert. What do barbers do beside cutting hair?"

"They try and sell one hairwash."

"No. No."

"They make conversation. They massage the scalp. They iron moustaches. They sometimes, I believe, cut people's corns."

"Oh Gilbert, something much simpler. Think, darling. Sh . . . Sh . . . "

162

"Shave?"

"Got it."

"But I shaved this morning. You're not asking me to shave again?"

"Oh, Gilbert, I think you're sweet. Is your chin a little bit rough, darling? How long after you shave does it get rough again? I *think* I should like it rough . . . " And she was off again on her galloping declaration of love.

More than once Mr. Pinfold — or rather a fanciful image of him derived from his books — had been the object of adolescent infatuation. Margaret's fervent, naïve tones reminded him of the letters which used to come, two a day usually for periods of a week or ten days, written in bed probably. They were confidences and avowals of love, bearing no address, asking no reciprocation or sign of recognition, the series ending as abruptly as it had begun. As a rule, he read none after the first, but here on the hostile *Caliban*, these guileless words uttered in Margaret's sweet, breathless tones fell softly on Mr. Pinfold's ear and he listened complacently. Indeed he began to relish these moments of unction which compensated for much of the ignorant abuse. That morning he had determined to change his cabin. That evening he was loth to cut himself off from this warm spring. But night wrought a change.

Mr. Pinfold did not dress or dine. He was very weary and he sat alone on deck until the passengers began to come up from dinner. Then he went to his cabin and for the first time for three days put on pyjamas, said his prayers, got into bed, turned off the light, composed himself for sleep, and slept.

He was awakened by Margaret's mother.

"Mr. Pinfold. Mr. Pinfold. Surely you haven't gone to sleep? Everyone is in bed now. Surely you haven't forgotten your promise to Margaret?"

"Mother, he didn't make any promise." Margaret's voice was tearful and strained, almost hysterical. "Not really. Not really what you could call a *promise*. Don't you see how awful it is for *me*, if you upset him now? He never *promised*."

"When I was young, dear, any man would be proud of a pretty girl taking notice of him. He wouldn't try and get out of it by pretending to be asleep."

"I asked for it. I expect I bore him. He's a man of the world. He's had hundreds of other girls, all sorts of horrible, fashionable, vicious old hags in London and Paris and Rome and New York. Why should he look at *me?* But I *do* love him so," and in her anguish she uttered the whimper which Mr. Pinfold had heard before in this ship on other lips.

"Don't cry, my dear. Mother will talk to him."

"Please, *please* not, Mother. I forbid you to interfere."

" 'Forbid' isn't a very nice word, is it, dear? You leave it to me. I'll talk to him. Mr. Pinfold. *Gilbert.* Wake up. Margaret's got something to say to you. He's awake now, dear, I know. Just tell her you're awake and listening, Gilbert."

"I'm awake and listening," said Mr. Pinfold.

"All right then, hold on — " she was like a telephone operator, Mr. Pinfold thought — "Margaret's going to speak to you. Come along, Margaret, speak up."

"I can't, Mother, I can't."

"You see, Gilbert, you've upset her. Tell her you love her. You do love her, don't you?"

"But I've never met her," said Mr. Pinfold desperately. "I'm sure she's a delightful girl, but I've never set eyes on her."

"Oh, Gilbert, Gilbert, that's not a very gallant thing to say, is it? Not really like you, not like the *real* you. You just pretend to be hard and worldly,

165

don't you? And you can't blame people if they take you at your own estimate. Everyone in the ship, you know, has been saying the most odious things about you. But I know better. Margaret wants to come and say good-night to you, Gilbert, but she's not sure you really love her. Just tell Mimi you love her, Gilbert."

"I can't, I don't," said Mr. Pinfold. "I'm sure your daughter is a most charming girl. It so happens I have never met her. It also happens that I have a wife. I love *her*."

"Oh, Gilbert, what a very middle-class thing to say!"

"He doesn't love me," wailed Margaret. "He doesn't love me any more."

"Gilbert, Gilbert, you're breaking my little girl's heart."

Mr. Pinfold was exasperated.

"I'm going to sleep now," he said. "Good-night."

"Margaret's coming to see you."

"Oh, shut up you old bitch," said Mr. Pinfold.

He should not have said it. The moment the words crossed his lips — or, rather, his mind — he knew it was not the right thing to say. The whole sturdy ship seemed to tremble with shock. There was a single piteous wail from Margaret, from her mother an inarticulate but plainly audible hiss of outrage, an attempt at bluster from the son: "My God, Peinfeld, you'll pay for that. If you think you can talk to my mother like — " And then, most unexpectedly, came a hearty chuckle from the General.

"Upon my soul, my dear, he called you an old bitch. Good for Peinfeld. That's something I've been longing to say to you for thirty years. You *are* an old bitch, you know, a thorough old bitch. Now perhaps you'll allow *me* to handle the situation. Clear out, the lot of you, I want to talk to my daughter. Come here, Meg, Peg o' my heart, my little Mimi." The voices became thick, the diction strangely Celtic as sentiment overpowered the military man. "You'll not be my little Mimi ever again any more after tonight and I'll not forget it. You're a woman now and you've set your heart on a man as a woman should. The choice is yours, not mine. He's old for you, but there's good in that. Many a young couple spend a wretched fortnight together through not knowing how to set about what has to be done. And an old man can show you better than a young one. He'll be gentler and kinder and cleaner; and then, when the right time comes, you in your turn can teach a

167

younger man — and that's how the art of love is
learned and the breed survives. I'd like dearly to be
the one myself to teach you, but you've made your
own choice and who's to grudge it you?"

"But, Father, he doesn't love me. He said not."

"Fiddlesticks. You're as pretty a girl as he'll meet
in a twelvemonth. There's certainly no one in this
ship to touch you and if he's the man I think, he'll
be feeling the need of an armful by now. Go in and
get him, lass. How do you think your mother got
me? Not by waiting to be asked, I can tell you. She
was a soldier's daughter. She always rode straight at
her fences. She rode straight at me, I can tell you.
Don't forget you're a soldier's daughter too. If you
want this fellow Pinfold, go in and take him. But
for God's sake come on parade looking like a soldier.
Get yourself cleaned up. Wash your face, brush your
hair, take your clothes off."

Margaret went obediently to her cabin. There she
was joined by her friend, several friends, it seemed,
a whole choir of bridesmaids who chanted an
epithalamium as they disrobed her and tired her
hair.

Mr. Pinfold listened with conflicting resentment
and fascination. He was a man accustomed to his

168

own preferences and decisions. It seemed to him that Margaret's parents were being officious and presumptuous, were making altogether too free with his passions. He had never, even in his bachelor days, been a strenuous philanderer.

Abroad, especially in remote places, he used to patronize brothels with the curiosity of a traveller who sought to taste all flavours of the exotic. In England he was rather constant and rather romantic in his affections. Since marriage he had been faithful to his wife. He had, since his acceptance of the laws of the Church, developed what approximated to a virtuous disposition; a reluctance to commit deliberate grave sins, which was independent of the fear of hell; he had assumed a personality to which such specifically forbidden actions were inappropriate. And yet amorous expectations began to stir in Mr. Pinfold. That acquired restraint and dignity of his had suffered some hard knocking about during the last few days. Margaret's visit was exciting. He started to plan her reception.

The cabin with its two narrow bunks was ill designed for such purposes. He began by tidying it, putting away his clothes and straightening the bed.

169

He succeeded only in making it look unoccupied. She would enter by that door. She must not find him reclining like a pasha. He must be on his feet. There was one chair only. Should he offer it to her? Should he draw her down to sit beside him on the bunk? There was a wooden board extending for half its length, convenient in rough weather, awkwardly placed for the operation he had in mind. Somehow he must dispose her, supine, on the bunk. For the opening phase her upper parts should be in the open space, her lower enclosed. He moved the pillows from the head to the foot of the bunk. He would be able to kneel beside her and so begin the conventional preliminary caresses. But how to get her there silently and gracefully. How to shift her? Was she portable? He wished that he knew her dimensions.

He took off his pyjamas and hung them in his cupboard, put on his dressing gown, and sat in the chair facing the door, waiting, while the folk-ritual of Margaret's preparations filled the cabin with music. As he waited his mood changed. Doubt and dismay intruded on his loving fancies. What on earth was he up to? What was he letting himself in for? He thought with disgust of Clutton-Cornforth and his tedious succession of joyless, purposeful seductions. He thought of his own enfeebled condition. "Feeling the need of an armful" indeed! Would he be able to sustain his interest during all the patient exploration required of him? Then as he gazed at the tidy bunk, he filled it with delicate, shrinking, yielding, yearning nudity, with a nymph by Boucher or Fragonard; and his mood changed again. Let her come. Let her come speedily. He was strongly armed for the encounter.

But Margaret did not hurry. The attendant virgins completed their services. She was inspected by both parents.

"Oh my darling, my own. You're so young. Are you sure? Are you quite sure you love him? You can always turn back. It's not too late. I shall never see you again as I am seeing you now, my innocent daughter."

"Yes, Mother, I love him."

"Be kind to her, Gilbert. You have not been kind to me. You used an expression to me that I never expected to hear on a man's lips. I meant never to speak to you again. But this is no moment for pride. My daughter's happiness is in your hands. Treat her *husbandly*. I'm entrusting something very precious to you. . . . "

171

And the General: "That's my beauty. Go and take what's coming to you. Listen, my Peg, you know what you're in for, don't you?"

"Yes, Father, I think so."

"It's always a surprise. You may think you know it all on paper, but like everything else in life it's never quite what you expect when it comes to action. There's no going back now. Come and see me when it's all over. I'll be waiting up to hear the report. In you go, bless you."

But still the girl delayed.

"Gilbert, Gilbert. Do you want me?" she asked. "Really and truly?"

"Yes, of course, come along."

"Say something sweet to me."

"I'll be sweet enough when you get here."

"Come and fetch me."

"Where are you?"

"Here. Just outside your cabin."

"Well, come along in. I've left the door open."

"I can't. I can't. You've got to come and fetch me."

"Oh, don't be such a little ass. I've been sitting here for goodness knows how long. Come in if you're coming. If you're not, I want to go back to bed."

At this Margaret broke into weeping and her

mother said: "Gilbert, that wasn't kind. It wasn't like you. You love her. She loves you. Can't you understand? A young girl; the first time; woo her, Gilbert, coax her. She's a little wild, woodland thing."

"What the hell's going on?" asked the General. "You ought to be in position by now. Haven't had a sitrep. Isn't the girl over the start line?"

"Oh, Father, I can't. *I can't.* I thought I could, but I *can't.*"

"Something's gone wrong, Pinfold. Find out. Send out patrols."

"Go and find her, Gilbert. Lure her in, tenderly, *husbandly.* She's just there waiting for you."

Rather crossly Mr. Pinfold strode into the empty corridor. He could hear Glover snoring. He could hear Margaret weeping quite close to him. He looked in the bathroom; not there. He looked round each corner, up and down the stairs; not there. He even looked in the lavatories, men's and women's; not there. Still the sobbing continued piteously. He returned to his cabin, fixed the door open on its hook and drew the curtain. He was overcome by weariness and boredom.

"I'm sorry, Margaret," he said, "I'm too old to start

173

playing hide and seek with schoolgirls. If you want to come to bed with me, you'll have to come and join me there."

He put on his pyjamas and lay down, pulling the blankets up to his chin. Presently he stretched out his arm and turned off the light. Then the passage light was disturbing. He shut the door. He rolled over on his side and lay between sleep and waking. Just as he was falling into unconsciousness he heard his door open and quickly shut. He opened his eyes too late to see the momentary gleam of light from the corridor. He heard slippered feet scurrying away and Margaret's despairing wail.

"I did go to him. I did. I did. I did. And when I got there he was lying in the dark snoring."

"Oh, my Margaret, my daughter. You should never have gone. It was all your father's fault."

"Sorry about that, Peg," said the General. "False appreciation."

The last voice Mr. Pinfold heard before he fell asleep was Goneril's: "Snoring? Shamming. Gilbert knew he wasn't up to it. He's impotent, aren't you, Gilbert? Aren't you?"

"It was Glover snoring," said Mr. Pinfold, but nobody seemed to hear him.

174

-◦[7]◦-

The Villains Unmasked — but Not Foiled

MR. PINFOLD did not sleep for very long. He awoke as usual when the men began washing the deck overhead, and he woke with the firm resolution of changing his cabin that day. His bond with Margaret was severed. He wished to be rid of the whole set of them and to sleep in peace in a cabin free of electrical freaks. He resolved, too, to move from the Captain's table. He had never wished to sit there. Anyone who coveted the place was welcome to it. Mr. Pinfold was going to be strictly private for the rest of the voyage.

This resolution was confirmed by the last of the many communications that had come to him in that cabin.

175

Shortly before the breakfast hour, the device brought him into contact with what he might have supposed would be its most natural source, the wireless office; he found himself listening not as before to the normal traffic of the ship, but to the conversation of the wireless operator; and this man was entertaining a party of early-risers, the bright young people, by reading to them the text of Mr. Pinfold's own messages.

" '*Everyone in ship most helpful. Love Gilbert.*' "

"That's a good one."

"Everyone?"

"I wonder if poor Gilbert thinks that now?"

"*Love.* Love from Gilbert. That's funny."

"Show us some more."

"Strictly speaking, you know, I oughtn't to. They're supposed to be confidential."

"Oh, come off it, Sparks."

"Well, this is rather rich. '*Entirely cured. All love.*' "

"Cured? Ha. Ha."

"*Entirely* cured."

"Our Gilbert *entirely cured!* Yes, that's delicious. Oh, Sparks, read us some more."

"I've never known a chap spend so much on

radiograms. They're mostly just about money and often he was so drunk I couldn't read what he'd written. There are an awful lot just refusing invitations. Oh, here's a good series. '*Kindly arrange immediate luxury private bath. Kindly investigate wanton inefficiency your office.*' He sent out dozens of those."

"Thank God for our Gilbert. What should we do without him?"

"Was his luxury private bath inefficient?"

" 'Wanton' is good coming from Gilbert. Does he wanton in his bath?"

To Mr. Pinfold this little scene was different in kind from the earlier annoyances. The bright young people had gone too far. It was one thing to play practical jokes on him; it was something quite else to read confidential messages. They had put themselves outside the law. Mr. Pinfold left his cabin for the dining-saloon with set purpose. He would put them on a charge.

He met the Captain making his morning round.

"Captain Steerforth, may I speak to you for a moment?"

"Surely." The Captain paused.

"In your cabin?"

"Yes, if you want to. I shall be through in ten minutes. Come up then. Or is it very urgent?"

"It can wait ten minutes."

Mr. Pinfold climbed to the cabin behind the bridge. Few personal additions embellished the solid ship's furniture. There were family photographs in leather frames; an etching of an English cathedral on the panelled wall which might have been the Captain's property or the company's; some pipes in a rack. Mr. Pinfold could not imagine this place the scene of orgy, outrage or plot.

Presently the Captain returned.

"Well, sir, and what can I do for you?"

"First, I want to know whether radiograms sent from your ship are confidential documents?"

"I'm sorry. I'm afraid I don't understand you."

"Captain Steerforth, since I came on board I have sent out a large number of messages of an entirely private character. This morning, early, there were a group of passengers reading them aloud in the wireless room."

"Well, we can easily get the facts about that. How many of these radiograms were there?"

"I don't know exactly. About a dozen."

178

"And when did you send them?"

"At various times during the early days of the voyage."

Captain Steerforth looked perplexed. "This is only our fifth day out, you know," he said.

"Oh," said Mr. Pinfold, disconcerted, "are you quite sure?"

"Yes, of course I'm sure."

"It seems longer."

"Well, come along to the office and we'll look into the matter."

The wireless room was only two doors from the Captain's cabin.

"This is Mr. Pinfold, a passenger."

"Yes, sir. We've seen him before."

"He wants to inquire about some radiograms he sent."

"We can easily check on that, sir. We've had practically no private traffic." He opened a file at his side and said: "Yes. Here we are. The day before yesterday. It went out within an hour of being handed in."

He showed Mr. Pinfold's holograph: *"Entirely cured. All love."*

"But the others?" said Mr. Pinfold bewildered.

179

"There were no others, sir."

"A dozen or more."

"Only this one. I should know, I can assure you."

"There was one I sent at Liverpool, the evening I came on board."

"That would have gone by Post Office Telegraph, sir."

"And you wouldn't have a copy here?"

"No, sir."

"Then how," said Mr. Pinfold, "was it possible for a group of passengers to read it aloud in this office at eight o'clock this morning?"

"Quite impossible," said the wireless operator. "I was on duty myself at that time. There were no passengers here."

He and the Captain exchanged glances.

"Does that satisfy all your questions, Mr. Pinfold?" asked the Captain.

"Not quite. May I come back to your cabin?"

"If you wish it."

When they were seated Mr. Pinfold said: "Captain Steerforth, I am the victim of a practical joke."

"Something of the sort, it seems," said the Captain.

"Not for the first time. Ever since I came on board this ship — you say it has only been five days?"

180

"Four actually."

"Ever since I came on board, I have been the victim of hoaxes and threats. Mind you I am not making any accusation. I don't know the names of these people. I don't even know what they look like. I am *not* asking for an official investigation — yet. What I do know is that the leaders comprise a family of four."

"I don't believe we have any families on board," said the Captain, taking the passenger list off his desk, "except the Angels. I hardly think they're the sort of people to play practical jokes on anyone. A very quiet family."

"There are several people travelling who aren't on that list."

"No one, I assure you."

"Fosker, for one."

Captain Steerforth turned the pages. "No," he said. "No Fosker."

"And that dark little man who used to sit alone in the dining saloon."

"Him? I know him well. He often travels with us. Mr. Murdoch — here he is on the list."

Baffled, Mr. Pinfold turned to another course suggested by Mr. Murdoch's solitary meals.

181

"Another thing, Captain. I greatly appreciate the honour of being invited to sit at your table in the dining-saloon. But the truth is I'm not fit for human society, just at the moment. I've been taking some grey pills — pretty strong stuff, for rheumatism, you know. I'm really better alone. So if you won't think it rude . . . "

"Sit where you like, Mr. Pinfold. Just tell the chief steward."

"Please understand I am not going because of any pressure from outside. It is simply that I am not well."

"I quite understand, Mr. Pinfold."

"I reserve the right to return if I feel better."

"Please sit exactly where you like, Mr. Pinfold. Is that all you wanted to say?"

"No. There's another thing. The cabin I'm in. You ought to get the wiring seen to. I don't know whether you know it, but I can often hear anything that's being said up here, on the bridge and in other parts of the ship."

"I didn't know," said Captain Steerforth. "That is most unusual."

"They've used this defect in their practical jokes. It's most disturbing. I should like to change cabins."

"That should be easy. We have two or three vacant. If you'll tell the purser . . . Is *that* everything, Mr. Pinfold?"

"Yes," said Mr. Pinfold. "Thank you very much. I am most grateful to you. And you *do* understand about my changing tables? You don't think it rude?"

"No offence whatever, Mr. Pinfold. Good morning."

Mr. Pinfold left the Captain far from content with his interview. It seemed to him that he had said too much or too little. But he had achieved certain limited objectives and he set about his business with the purser and chief steward with alacrity. He was given the very table where Mr. Murdoch had sat. Of several cabins he chose a small one near the verandah-bar which gave immediate access to the promenade deck. Here, he was sure, he would be safe from physical attack.

He returned to his old cabin to direct the removal of his possessions. The voices began at once but he was very busy with the English-speaking steward and did not listen until he had seen his clothes and belongings packed and carried away. Then briefly he surveyed the scene of his suffering and lent them his ears. He was gratified to find that, however incomplete it looked to him, his morning's work had dismayed his enemies.

"Dirty little sneak — " there was a note of fear in Goneril's hatred that morning — "what have you been saying to the Captain? We'll get even with you. Have you forgotten the three-eight rhythm? Did you tell him our names? Did you? Did you?"

Margaret's brother was positively conciliatory: "Look here, Gilbert, old boy, we don't want to bring other people into our business, do we? We can settle it between ourselves, can't we, Gilbert?"

Margaret was reproachful; not because of the drama of the night; all that storm of emotion seemed to have passed, leaving no more trace than thunderclouds in the blue of summer. Indeed in all their subsequent acquaintance she never mentioned that fiasco; she chid him instead gently for his visit to the Captain. "It's *against the Rules*, darling, don't you see. We *must* all play by the Rules."

"I'm not playing at all."

"Oh yes, darling, you are. We all are. We can't help ourselves. And it's a Rule that no one else must be told. If there's anything you don't understand, ask me."

Poor waif, Mr. Pinfold thought, she has kept bad

184

company and been corrupted. After the embarrassments of the night Margaret had forfeited his trust, but he loved her a little and felt it unmannerly to be leaving her flat, as he planned to do. It had proved easy to move out of their reach. They had confided too much, these aggressive young people, in their mechanical toy. And now he was breaking it.

"Margaret," he said, "I don't know anything about your rules and I am not playing any game with any of you. But I should like to see you. Come and join me on deck any time you like."

"Darling, you know I long to. But I can't, can I? You do see, don't you?"

"No," said Mr. Pinfold, "frankly I don't see. I leave it to you. I'm off now," and he left the haunted cabin for the last time.

It was the social hour of noon, when the sweepstake was paid and the cocktails ordered. From his new cabin, where his new steward was unpacking, he could hear the chatter from the bar. He stood alone thinking how smoothly he had made the transition.

He repeated to himself all that had been said in the Captain's cabin: ". . . *no families on board except the Angels?*" Angel. And suddenly Mr. Pinfold understood, not everything, but the heart of the mystery. Angel, the quizzical man from the B.B.C. " — *not wires, darling. Wireless*" — Angel, the man with the technical skill to use the defects of the *Caliban's* communications, perhaps to cause them. Angel, the man with the beard — *"What do barbers do besides cut hair?"* — Angel, who had an aunt near Lychpole and could have heard from her the garbled gossip of the countryside. Angel, who had "half expected" Cedric Thorne to kill himself; Angel, who bore a grudge for the poor figure he had cut at Lychpole and had found Mr. Pinfold by chance alone and ill and defenceless, ripe for revenge. Angel was the villain, he and his sinister associate — mistress? colleague? — whom Mr. Pinfold had dubbed "Goneril." And Angel had gone too far. He was afraid now that his superiors in London might get wind of his escapade. And they would, too; Mr. Pinfold would see to that, when he returned to England. He might even write from the ship. If, as seemed probable, he was travelling on duty, the B.B.C. would have something to say to young Angel, bearded or shaven.

There were many passages in the story of the last few days that remained obscure under this new, bright light. Mr. Pinfold felt as though he had come to the end of an ingenious, old-fashioned detective novel which he had read rather inattentively. He knew the villain now and began turning back the pages to observe the clues he had missed.

It was not the first time in the *Caliban* that noon had brought an illusion of shadowless commonplace.

The change of cabin was not the tactical triumph Mr. Pinfold briefly supposed. He was like a commander whose attack "hit air." The post he had captured, which had seemed the key of the enemy's position, proved to be empty, a mere piece of deception masking an elaborate and strongly held system; the force he supposed routed was reinforced and ready for the counter-attack.

Mr. Pinfold discovered, before he went down to his first lonely luncheon, that Angel's range of action was not limited to the original cabin and the corner of the lounge. From some mobile point of control he could speak and listen in every part of the ship and in the following days Mr. Pinfold, wherever he stood, could hear, could not keep himself from hearing, everything that was said in Angel's headquarters. Living and moving and eating now quite alone, barely nodding to Glover and Mrs. Scarfield, Mr.

187

Pinfold listened and spoke only to his enemies and hour by hour, day by day, night by night, carefully assembled the intricate pieces of a plot altogether more modern and horrific than anything in the classic fictions of murder.

Mr. Pinfold's change of cabin had momentarily disconcerted Angel and his staff (there were about half a dozen of them, male and female, all young, basically identical with the three-eight orchestra); moreover it seemed likely that the scare of the day before, when it was put about the ship that he had gone overboard, was genuine enough. At any rate Angel's first concern was that Mr. Pinfold should be kept under continual observation. Immediate reports were made to headquarters of his every move. These reports were concise and factual.

"Gilbert has sat down at his table. . . . He's reading the menu. . . . He's ordering wine. . . . He's ordered a plate of cold ham."

When he moved he was passed on to relays of observers.

"Gilbert coming up to main deck. Take over, B."

"O.K., A. Gilbert now approaching door on port side, going out onto deck. Take over, C."

"O.K., B. Gilbert walking the deck anti-clockwise.

188

He's approaching the main door, starboard side. Over to you, B."

"He's sitting down with a book."

"O.K., B. Stay on duty in the lounge. Report any move. I'll have you relieved at three."

Mr. Pinfold, looking from one to another of the occupants of the lounge, wondered which was B. Later it transpired that about half the passengers had been recruited by Angel for observation duties. They considered it an innocuous parlour game. Of the rest some knew nothing of what was afoot — this group included Glover and the Scarfields — others thought the whole thing silly. The inner circle manned the staff office, where reports were collated and inquiries instigated. Every few hours a conference was held at which Angel collected and discussed the notes of his observers, drafted them into a coherent report and gave them to a girl to be typed. He maintained a rollicking good humour and zest.

"Great stuff. Splendid . . . My word, Gilbert's given himself away here. . . . Most valuable . . . We could do with a little more detail on these points. . . . "

Anything Mr. Pinfold had said or done or thought,

that day or in his past life, seemed significant. Angel was mocking, but appreciative. At intervals two older men — not the Generals, but men more akin to them than to the boisterous youngsters — subjected Mr. Pinfold to direct questioning. This inquisition, it appeared, was the essence of the enterprise. It was prosecuted whenever Mr. Pinfold sat in the lounge or lay in his cabin, and so curious was he about the motives and mechanics of the thing that for the first twenty-four hours he, to some extent, collaborated. The inquisitors, it seemed, possessed a huge but incomplete and wildly inaccurate dossier covering the whole of Mr. Pinfold's private life. It was their task to fill the gaps. In manner they were part barristers, part bureaucrats.

"Where were you in January 1929, Pinfold?"

"I really don't know."

"Perhaps I can refresh your memory. I have here a letter from you written at Mena House Hotel, Cairo. Were you in Egypt in 1929?"

"Yes, I believe I was."

"And what were you doing there?"

"Nothing."

"Nothing? That won't do, Pinfold. I want a better answer than that."

190

"I was just travelling."

"Of course you were travelling. You could hardly get to Egypt without travelling, could you? I want the truth, Pinfold. *What were you doing* in Egypt in 1929?"

On another occasion: "How many pairs of shoes do you possess?"

"I really don't know."

"You *must* know. Would you say a dozen?"

"Yes, I daresay."

"We have you down here as possessing ten."

"Perhaps."

"Then why did you tell me a dozen, Pinfold? He did say a dozen, didn't he?"

"Quite distinctly."

"I don't like this, Pinfold. You have to be truthful. Only the truth can help you."

Sometimes they turned to more immediate topics.

"On more than one occasion you have complained of suffering from the effects of some grey pills. Where did they come from?"

"My doctor."

"Do you suppose he manufactured them himself?"

"No, I suppose not."

"Well then, answer my question properly. Where did those pills come from?"

"I really don't know. Some chemist, I suppose."

"Exactly. Would it surprise you to hear they came from Wilcox and Bredworth?"

"Not particularly."

"*Not particularly*, Pinfold? I must warn you to be careful. Don't you know that Wilcox and Bredworth are one of the most respected firms in the country?"

"Yes."

"And you accuse them of purveying dangerous drugs?"

"I expect they manufacture great quantities of poison."

"You mean you accuse Wilcox and Bredworth of conspiring with your doctor to poison you?"

"Of course I don't."

"Then what *do* you mean?"

Sometimes they made in their stern, precise voices accusations as fantastic as those of the hooligans and the gossips. They pressed him for information about the suicide of a staff-officer in the Middle East — a man who to the best of Mr. Pinfold's knowledge had ended the war healthily and prosperously — which they attributed to Mr. Pinfold's malice. They brought

192

up the old charges of the eviction of Hill and of Mrs. Pinfold senior's pauper's funeral. They examined him about a claim he had never made, to be the nephew of an Anglican bishop.

Once or twice during these days Angel organized a rag, but since Mr. Pinfold could hear the preparations, he was not dismayed as he had been by the previous exercises.

Early one morning he heard Angel announce: "We will mount Operation Storm today," and as soon as the ship came to life and the passengers began their day, all conversations, when they passed Mr. Pinfold, or he them, was about a gale warning. ". . . The Captain says we're coming right into it."

"One of the worst storms he's ever known in the Mediterranean . . . "

The day was bright and calm. Mr. Pinfold had no fear — if anything he had rather a relish — for rough weather. After an hour of this charade Angel called it off. "No good," he said. "Operation cancelled. Gilbert isn't scared."

"He's a good sailor," said Margaret.

"He doesn't mind missing his lunch," said Goneril. "The food isn't good enough for him."

"Operation Stock Exchange," said Angel.

193

This performance was even more fatuous than its predecessor. The method was the same, a series of conversations designed for him to hear. The subject was a financial slump which had suddenly thrown the stock-markets of the world into chaos. As they sauntered past or sat over their knitting the passengers dutifully recounted huge falls in the prices of stocks and shares in the world capital cities, the suicide of financiers, the closing of banks and corporations. They quoted figures. They named the companies which had failed. All this, even had he believed it, would have been of very remote interest to Mr. Pinfold.

"They say Mr. Pinfold's fortune is entirely wiped out," said Mrs. Benson to Mrs. Cockson (these ladies had now resumed their mother tongue).

Mr. Pinfold had no fortune. He owned a few fields, a few pictures, a few valuable books, his own copyrights. At the bank he had a small overdraft. He had never in his life put out a penny at interest. The rudimentary technicalities of finance were Greek to him. It was very odd, he thought, that these people could go to so much trouble to investigate his affairs and know so little about them.

The Villains Unmasked — but Not Foiled

"Operation cancelled," announced Angel at length.

"What went wrong?"

"I wish I knew. Gilbert is no longer responding to treatment. We had him on the run in the early days. Now he seems punch-drunk."

"He's in a sort of daze."

"He's not sleeping enough."

This was indeed true. Since he finished his sleeping-draught Mr. Pinfold had seldom had more than an hour at a time of uneasy dozing. The nights were a bad time for him. He would sit in the lounge, alone in his dinner jacket, observing his fellow passengers, distracted a little by their activities from the voices of his enemies, trying to decide which were his friends, which were neutral, until the last of them had gone below and the lights were turned down. Then, knowing what to expect, he would go to his cabin and undress. He had given up any attempt at saying his prayers; the familiar, hallowed words provoked a storm of blasphemous parody from Goneril.

He lay down expecting little rest. Angel had in his headquarters an electric instrument which showed Mr. Pinfold's precise state of consciousness.

195

It consisted, Mr. Pinfold surmised, of a glass tube containing two parallel lines of red light which continually drew together or moved apart like telegraph wires seen from a train. They approached one another as he grew drowsy and, when he fell asleep, crossed. A duty officer followed their fluctuations.

" . . . Wide awake . . . now he's getting sleepy . . . they're almost touching . . . a single line . . . they're going to cross . . . no, wide awake again . . . " And when he awoke after his brief spells of insensibility, his first sensation was always the voice of the observer: "Gilbert's awake again. Fifty-one minutes."

"That's better than the time before."

"But it isn't enough."

One night they tried to soothe him by playing a record specially made by Swiss scientists for the purpose. These savants had decided from experiments made in a sanatorium for neurotic industrial workers that the most soporific noises were those of a factory. Mr. Pinfold's cabin resounded to the roar and clang of machinery.

"You bloody fools," he cried in exasperation, "*I'm* not a factory worker. You're driving me mad."

"No, no, Gilbert, you *are* mad already," said the duty officer. "We're driving you sane."

The hubbub continued until Angel came on his round of inspection.

"Gilbert not asleep yet? Let me see the log. *'0312 hours. You bloody fools, I'm not a factory worker.'* Well, nor he is. *'You're driving me mad.'* I believe we are. Turn off that record. Give him something rural."

From then for a long time nightingales sang to Mr. Pinfold but still he did not sleep. He stepped out on deck and leaned on the rail.

"Go on, Gilbert. Jump. In you go," said Goneril. Mr. Pinfold did not feel the smallest temptation to obey. "Water-funk."

"I know all about that actor, you know," said Mr. Pinfold. "The one who was a friend of Angel's and hanged himself in his dressing-room."

This was the first time that he disclosed his knowledge of Angel's identity. The effect was immediate. All Angel's assumed good humour was dispelled. "Why do you call me Angel?" he asked fiercely. "What the devil do you mean by it?"

"It's your name. I know exactly what you are doing for the B.B.C." — this was bluff — "I know exactly what you did to Cedric Thorne. I know exactly what you are trying to do to me."

197

"Liar. You don't know anything."

"Liar," said Goneril.

"I told you," said Margaret. "Gilbert's no fool."

Silence fell on the headquarters. Mr. Pinfold returned to his bunk, lay down and slept until the steward came in with his tea. Angel spoke to him at once. He was in a chastened mood. "Look here, Gilbert, you've got us all wrong. What we're doing is nothing to do with the B.B.C. It's a private enterprise entirely. And as for Cedric — that wasn't our fault. He came to us too late. We did everything we could for him. He was a hopeless case. Why don't you answer? Can't you hear me, Gilbert? Why don't you answer?"

Mr. Pinfold held his peace. He was getting near to a full explanation.

Mr. Pinfold was never able to give a completely coherent account either to himself or to anyone else of how he finally unravelled the mystery. He heard so much, directly and indirectly; he reasoned so closely; he followed so many false clues and reached so many absurd conclusions; but at length he was satisfied that he knew the truth. He then sat down and wrote about it at length to his wife.

The Villains Unmasked — but Not Foiled

Darling,

As I said in my telegram I am quite cured of my aches and pains. In that way the trip has been a success but this has not proved a happy ship and I have decided to get off at Port Said and go on by aeroplane.

Do you remember the tick with a beard who came to Lychpole from the B.B.C. He is on board with a team bound for Aden. They are going to make recordings of Arab dance music. The tick is called Angel. He has shaved his beard. That is why I didn't spot him at first. He has some of his family with him — rather a nice sister — travelling I suppose for pleasure. They seem to be cousins of a lot of our neighbours. You might enquire. These B.B.C. people have made themselves a great nuisance to me on board. They have got a lot of apparatus with them, most of it new and experimental. They have something which is really a glorified form of Reggie Graves-Upton's Box. I shall never laugh at the poor Bruiser again. There is a great deal in it. More in fact than he imagines. Angel's Box is able to speak and to hear. In fact I spend most of my days and nights carrying on conversations with people I never see. They are trying to psychoanalyse me. I know this sounds absurd. The Germans at the end of the war were developing this Box for the examination of prisoners. The Russians have perfected it. They don't need any of the old physical means of per-

suasion. They can see into the minds of the most
obdurate. The Existentialists in Paris first started
using it for psychoanalysing people who would not
voluntarily submit to treatment. They first break the
patient's nerve by acting all sorts of violent scenes
which he thinks are really happening. They confuse
him until he doesn't distinguish between natural
sounds and those they induce. They make all kinds
of preposterous accusations against him. Then when
they get him in a receptive mood they start on their
psychoanalysis. As you can imagine it's a hellish
invention in the wrong hands. Angel's are very much
the wrong hands. He's an amateur and a conceited
ass. That young man who came to the hotel with my
tickets was there to measure my "Life-Waves." I
should have thought they could equally well have
got them on board. Perhaps there is some particular
gadget they have to get in London for each person.
I don't know. There is still a good deal about the
whole business I don't know. When I get back I will
make enquiries. I'm not the first person they've tried
it on. They drove an actor to suicide. I rather sus-
pect they've been at work on poor Roger Stillingfleet. In fact I think we shall find a number of our
friends who have behaved oddly lately have suffered
from Angel.

Anyway they have had no success with me. I've
seen through them. All they have done is to stop my
working. So I am leaving them. I shall go straight

to the Galleface in Colombo and look round from there for a quiet place in the hills. I'll telegraph when I arrive which should be about the time you get this letter.

All love,

G

"Gilbert," said Angel, "you can't send that letter."

"I am certainly going to — by air mail from Port Said."

"It's going to make trouble."

"I hope so."

"You don't understand the importance of the work we're doing. Did you see *The Cocktail Party?* Do you remember the second act? We are like the people in that, a little band doing good, sworn to secrecy, working behind the scenes everywhere — "

"You're a pretentious busy-body."

"Look here, Gilbert — "

"And who the devil said you might use my Christian name?"

"Gilbert."

"Mr. Pinfold to you."

"Mr. Pinfold, I admit we've not handled your case properly. We'll leave you in peace if you'll destroy that letter."

201

"*I* am leaving *you*, my good Angel. The question does not arise."

Goneril cut in: "We'll give you hell for this, Gilbert. We'll get you and you know it. We'll never let you go. We've got you."

"Oh, shut up," said Mr. Pinfold.

He felt himself master of the field; caught unawares, with unfamiliar barbarous weapons, treacherously ambushed when, as it were, he was under the cover of the Red Cross, he had rallied and routed the enemy. Their grand strategy had been utterly frustrated. All they could do now was snipe.

This they did continuously during the last twenty-four hours of the voyage. Mr. Pinfold went about his business in a babble of jeering, threatening, cajoling voices. He gave notice to the purser of his intention of leaving the ship and sent a message by wireless engaging an air passage to Colombo.

"You can't go, Gilbert. They won't let you off the ship. The doctor has you under observation. He'll keep you in a home because you're mad, Gilbert. . . . You haven't the money. You can't hire a car. . . . Your passport expired last week. . . . They won't take travellers' cheques in Egypt. . . . " "He's got dollars, the beast." "Well, that's criminal. He ought to have declared them. They'll get him for that." "They won't let you through the military zone, Gilbert." (This was in 1954.) "The army will turn you back. Egyptian terrorists are bombing private cars on the canal road."

Mr. Pinfold fought back with the enemy's weapons. He was obliged to hear all they said. They were obliged to hear him. They could not measure his emotions but every thought which took verbal shape in his mind was audible in Angel's headquarters and they were unable, it seemed, to disconnect their Box. Mr. Pinfold set out to wear them down with sheer boredom. He took a copy of *Westward Ho!* from the ship's library and read it very slowly hour by hour. At first Goneril attempted to correct his pronunciation. At first Angel pretended to find psychological significance in the varying emphasis he gave to different words. But after an hour or so they gave up these pretences and cried in frank despair: "Gilbert, for God's sake stop."

Then Mr. Pinfold tormented them in his turn by making gibberish of the text, reading alternate lines, alternate words, reading backwards, until they pleaded for a respite. Hour after hour Mr. Pinfold remorselessly read on.

On his last evening he felt magnanimous towards all except Angel and Goneril. Word had got round the passengers that he was leaving them and as he sauntered among them he noted genuine regret in the scraps of talk he overheard.

"Is it really because of that game of Mr. Angel's?" he heard Mrs. Benson ask.

"He's very much annoyed with all of us."

"You can hardly blame him. I'm sorry now I took any part in it."

"It wasn't really very funny. I never saw the point really."

"What's more we've cost him a lot of money. He may be able to afford it, but it's unfair, all the same."

"I never believed half they said about him."

"I wish I'd got to know him. I believe he's really very nice."

"He's a very distinguished man and we've behaved like a lot of badly brought up children."

There was no hatred or ridicule now in any of their conversations. That evening before dinner, he joined the Scarfields.

"In a couple of days it will be getting hot," she said.

"I shan't be here."

"Not here? I thought you were going to Co lombo?"

He explained the change of plan.

"Oh, what a pity," she said with an unmistakable innocence. "It's only after Port Said that one ever really gets to know people."

"I think I'll dine at your table tonight."

"Do. We've missed you."

So Mr. Pinfold returned to the Captain's table and ordered champagne for them all. None except the Captain knew of his imminent departure. Throughout all the tumult of the journey this little group had remained isolated and unaware of what was afoot. Mr. Pinfold was still not sure of the Captain. That quiet sea-dog had turned a Nelson eye on proceedings far beyond the scope of his imagination.

"I'm sorry we shan't have you with us, particularly now you are feeling so much better," he said, raising his glass. "I hope you have a comfortable flight."

"Urgent business, I suppose?" said Glover.

"Just impatience," said Mr. Pinfold.

He remained with the group. Glover gave him advice about tailors in Colombo and cool hotels in the hills suitable for literary work. When they broke up, Mr. Pinfold said good-bye, for the *Caliban* was

205

due in harbour early and all would be busy next morning.

On his way to his cabin he met the dark figure of Mr. Murdoch, who stopped and spoke to him. His manner was genial and his voice richly redolent of the industrial North.

"Purser tells me you're landing tomorrow," he said. "So am I. How do you reckon to get to Cairo?"

"I haven't really thought. Train, I suppose."

"Ever been in an Egyptian train? Filthy dirty and slow. I tell you what, my firm's sending a car for me. I'd be glad of your company."

So it was arranged they should travel together.

The night still belonged to Angel and Goneril. "Don't trust Murdoch," they whispered. "Murdoch is your enemy." There was no peace in the cabin and Mr. Pinfold remained on deck watching for the poor little pharos of Port Said, recognized its beam, saw the pilot come aboard with a launchful of officials in tarbooches, saw the water-front come clear in view populous even at that hour with touts and scarab-sellers.

In the hubbub of early morning and the successive interviews with port officials Mr. Pinfold was intermittently aware that Goneril and Angel were still jabbering, still impotently trying to obstruct. Only when, at last he went down the gangway, did they fall silent. Mr. Pinfold had been to Port Said often before. He had never expected to feel affection for the place. That day he did. He watched patiently while unshaven, smoking officials examined him, his passport and his baggage. He cheerfully paid a number of absurd impositions. An English agent of Mr. Murdoch's company warned them:

" . . . Pretty tricky drive at the moment. Only last week there was a chap hired a car to go to Cairo. The native driver left the road just after Ismailia and turned into a village. He was set on, all his luggage pinched. They even took his clothes. Not a stitch on when the police picked him up. And all they said was he ought to consider himself lucky they hadn't cut his throat."

Mr. Pinfold did not care. He posted his letter to his wife. He and Murdoch drank a bottle of beer at a café and suffered their boots to be cleaned two or three times. The funnels of the *Caliban* were plainly to be seen from where he sat, but no voices came from her. Then he and Murdoch drove away out of sight of the unhappy ship.

The road to Cairo was more warlike than he had known it ten years back when Rommel was at the gates. They passed through lanes of barbed wire, halted and showed his passport at numerous barriers, crept in dust behind convoys of army trucks, each with a sentry crouched on the tail-board with a tommy-gun at the ready. There came a longer halt and closer scrutiny at the turning out of the Canal Zone, where swarthy, sullen English soldiers gave place to swarthy, sullen Egyptians in almost identical uniforms. Murdoch was a man of few words and Mr. Pinfold sat enveloped in his own impervious peace.

Once during the war he had gone on a parachute course which had ended ignominiously with his breaking a leg in his first drop, but he treasured as the most serene and exalted experience of his life the moment of liberation when he regained consciousness after the shock of the slip-stream. A quarter of a minute before he had crouched over the open man-hole in the floor of the machine, in dusk and deafening noise, trussed in harness, crowded by apprehensive fellow tyros. Then the despatching officer had signalled; down he had plunged into a moment of night, to come to himself in a silent, sunlit heaven, gently supported by what had seemed irksome bonds, absolutely isolated. There were other parachutes all round him holding other swaying bodies; there was an instructor on the ground bawling advice through a loud-speaker; but Mr. Pinfold felt himself free of all human communication, the sole inhabitant of a private, delicious universe. The rapture was brief. Almost at once he knew he was not floating but falling; the field leaped up at him; a few seconds later he was lying on grass entangled in cords, being shouted at, breathless, bruised, with a sharp pain in the shin. But in that moment of solitude prosaic, earthbound Mr. Pinfold had been one with hashish-eaters and Corybantes and Californian gurus, high on the back-stairs of mysticism. His mood on the road to Cairo was barely less ecstatic.

Cairo was still pocked and gutted by the recent riots. It was thronged with stamp dealers who had come for the sale of the royal collection. Mr. Pinfold had difficulty in finding a room. Murdoch obtained one for him. There was difficulty with his air passage and there too Murdoch helped. Finally on the second day, when Mr. Pinfold was provided by the concierge of his hotel with all the requisite documents

— including a medical certificate and a sworn statement, necessary for a halt in Arabia, that he was a Christian — and his departure was fixed for midnight, Murdoch invited him to dine with his business associates in Ghezira.

"They'll be delighted. They don't see many people from home these days. And to tell you the truth I'm glad to have a companion myself. I don't much like driving about alone after dark."

So they went to dinner in a block of expensive, modern flats. The lift was out of order. As they climbed the stairs they passed an Egyptian soldier squatting in a doorway flat, chewing nuts, with his rifle propped behind him.

"One of the old princesses," said Murdoch, "under house-arrest."

Host and hostess greeted them kindly. Mr. Pinfold looked about him. The drawing-room was furnished with the trophies of long residence in the East. On the chimney piece was the framed photograph of a peer in coronation-robes. Mr. Pinfold studied it.

"Surely that's Simon Dumbleton?"

"Yes, he's a great friend of ours. Do you know him?"

Before he could answer another voice broke in on that cosy scene.

"No, you don't, Gilbert," said Goneril. "Liar. Snob. You only pretend to know him because he's a lord."

◄8►

Pinfold Regained

M R. PINFOLD landed at Colombo three days later. He had spent one almost sleepless night in the aeroplane, where a pallid Parsee sprawled and grunted and heaved beside him; and a second equally wakeful alone in a huge, teetotal hotel in Bombay. Night and day Angel, Goneril and Margaret chattered to him in their several idioms. He was becoming like the mother of fractious children who had learned to go about her business with a mind closed to their utterances; except that he had no business. He could only sit hour after hour waiting in one place or another for meals he did not want. Sometimes from sheer boredom he spoke to Margaret and learned from her further details of the conspiracy.

"Are you still in the ship?"

"No. We got off at Aden."

"All of you?"

"All three."

"But the others?"

"There never were any others, Gilbert. Just my brother and sister-in-law and me. You saw our names in the passenger list, Mr. and Mrs. and Miss Angel. I thought you understood all that."

"But your mother and father?"

"They're in England, at home — quite near Lychpole."

"Never in the ship?"

"Darling, you are slow in the uptake. What you heard was my brother. He's really awfully good at imitations. That's how he first got taken on by the B.B.C."

"And Goneril is married to your brother? There was never anything between her and the Captain?"

"No, of course not. She's beastly but not like that. All *that* was part of the Plan."

"I think I'm beginning to understand. You must see it's all rather confusing." Mr. Pinfold puzzled his weary head over the matter, then gave it up and asked: "What are you doing in Aden?"

"Me? Nothing. The others have their work. It's awfully dull for me. May I talk to you sometimes?

213

I know I'm not a bit clever but I'll try not to be a bore. I do so want company."

"Why don't you go and see the mermaid?"

"I don't understand."

"There used to be a mermaid at Aden in a box in one of the hotels — stuffed."

"Don't tease, Gilbert."

"I'm not teasing. And anyway that comes pretty badly from a member of your family. *Tease* indeed."

"Oh, Gilbert, you don't understand. We were only trying to help you."

"Who the devil said I needed help?"

"Don't be cross, Gilbert; not with me anyway. And you did need help, you know. Often their plans work beautifully."

"Well, you must realize by now that it hasn't worked with me."

"Oh, no," said Margaret sadly. "It hasn't worked at all."

"Then why not leave me alone?"

"They never will now, because they hate you. And I never will, never. You see I love you so. Try not to hate me, darling."

From Cairo to Colombo he talked intermittently

to Margaret. To the Angels, husband and wife, he made no answer.

Ceylon was a new country to Mr. Pinfold but he had no sense of exhilaration on arrival. He was tired and sweaty. He was wearing the wrong clothes. His first act after leaving his luggage at the hotel was to seek the tailor Glover had recommended. The man promised to work all night and have three suits ready for him to try on next morning.

"You're too fat. You'll look ridiculous in them. They won't fit. . . . You can't afford them. . . . The tailor's lying. He won't make clothes for you," Goneril monotonously interpolated.

Mr. Pinfold returned to his hotel and wrote to his wife:

I have arrived safe and well. There does not seem to be much to see or do in Colombo. I will move as soon as I have some clothes. I rather doubt whether I shall get any work done. I had a disappointment leaving the ship. I thought I should get out of range of those psychoanalysts and their infernal Box. But not at all. They still annoy me with the whole length of India between us. As I write this letter they keep

215

*interrupting. It will be quite impossible to do any
of my book. There must be some way of cutting the
"vital waves." I think it might be worth consulting
Father Westmacott when I get back. He knows all
about existentialism and psychology and ghosts and
diabolic possession. Sometimes I wonder whether it
is not literally the Devil who is molesting me.*

He posted this by air mail. Then he sat on the
terrace watching the new cheap cars drive up and
away. Here, unlike Bombay, one could drink. He
drank bottled English beer. The sky darkened. A
thunderstorm broke. He moved from the terrace
into the lofty hall. To a man at Mr. Pinfold's time of
life few throngs comprise only strangers. In the busy
hall he was greeted by an acquaintance from New
York, a collector for one of the art galleries, on his
way to visit a ruined city on the other side of the
island. He asked Mr. Pinfold to join him.

At that moment a gentle servant appeared at his
side: "Mr. Peenfold, sir, cable."

It came from his wife and read: *"Implore you return immediately."*

It was not like Mrs. Pinfold to issue a summons
of this kind. Could she be ill? Or one of the children?
Had the house burned down? She would, surely?

have given some explanation. It occurred to Mr. Pinfold that she must be concerned on his account. That letter he had sent from Port Said, had it said anything to cause alarm? He answered: *"All well. Returning soon. Have written today. Off to the ruins,"* and rejoined his new companion. They dined together cheerfully, having many tastes and friends and memories in common. All that evening, though there was an undertone in his ears, Mr. Pinfold was oblivious of the Angels. Not till late, when he was alone in his room, did the voices break through. "We heard you, Gilbert. You were lying to that American. You've never stayed at Rhinebeck. You've never heard of Magnasco. You don't know Osbert Sitwell."

"Oh God," said Mr. Pinfold, "how you bore me!"

It was cooler among the ruins. There was refreshment in the leafy roads, in the spectacle of grey elephants and orange-robed, shaven-pated monks ambling meditatively in the dust. They stopped at rest-houses where they were greeted and zealously served by old servants of the British Raj. Mr. Pinfold enjoyed himself. On the way back they stopped at the shrine of Kandy and saw the Buddha's tooth ceremoniously exposed. This seemed to exhaust the

217

artistic resources of the island. The American was on his way farther east. They parted company four days later at the hotel in Colombo where they had met. Mr. Pinfold was alone once more and at a loose end. He found waiting for him a pile of clothes from the tailor and another cable from his wife: *"Both your letters received. Am coming to join you."*

It had been handed in at Lychpole that morning.

"He hates his wife," said Goneril. "She bores you, doesn't she, Gilbert? You don't want to go home, do you? You dread seeing her again."

That decided him. He cabled: *"Returning at once"* and set about his preparations.

The three suits were pale, pinkish buff ("How smart you look," cried Margaret); they were not entirely useless. He wore them on successive days, first in Colombo.

It was Sunday and he went to Mass for the first time since he had been struck ill. The voices followed him. The taxi took him first to the Anglican church. ". . . What's the difference, Gilbert? It's all nonsense anyway. You don't believe in God. There's no one here to show off to. No one will listen to your prayers — except us. *We* shall hear them. You're going to pray to be left alone, aren't you, Gilbert? Aren't you? But only we will hear and we won't let you alone. Never, Gilbert, never . . . " But when he reached the little Catholic church which, ironically enough, he found to be dedicated to St. Michael and the Angels, only Margaret followed him into the dusky, crowded interior. She knew the Mass and made the Latin responses in clear, gentle tones. Epistle and Gospel were read in the vernacular. There was a short sermon, during which Mr. Pinfold asked: "Margaret, are you a Catholic?"

"In a way."

"In what way?"

"That's something you mustn't ask."

Then she rose with him to recite the creed and later, at the sacring-bell, she urged: "Pray for them, Gilbert. They need prayers." But Mr. Pinfold could not pray for Angel and Goneril.

On Monday he arranged his passage. On Tuesday he spent another ineffably tedious night at Bombay. On Wednesday night at Karachi he changed back into winter clothes. Somewhere on the sea they may have passed the *Caliban*. They steered far clear of Aden. Across the Moslem world the voices of hate pursued Mr. Pinfold. It was when they reached Christendom that Angel changed his tune. At breakfast at Rome Mr. Pinfold addressed the waiter, who spoke rather good English, in rather bad Italian. It was an affectation which Goneril was quick to exploit.

"No spikka de Eenglish," she jeered. "Kissa da monk. *Dolce far niente.*"

"Shut up," said Angel sharply. "We've had enough of that. I've got to talk to Gilbert seriously. Listen, Gilbert, I've got a proposition to make."

But Mr. Pinfold would not answer.

Intermittently throughout the flight to Paris Angel attempted to open a discussion.

"Gilbert, do listen to me. We've got to come to some arrangement. Time's getting short. Gilbert, old boy, do be reasonable."

His tone changed from friendliness to cajolery, at length to a whine; the voice which had been so well-bred was now the underdog's voice which Mr. Pinfold remembered from their brief meeting at Lychpole.

"Do speak to him, Gilbert," Margaret pleaded. "He's really very worried."

"So he should be. If your miserable brother wants me to reply he can address me properly, as 'Mr. Pinfold,' or 'Sir.' "

"Very well, Mr. Pinfold, sir," said Angel.

"That's better. Now what have you to say?"

"I want to apologize. I've made a mess of the whole Plan."

"You certainly have."

"It was a serious scientific experiment. Then I let personal malice interfere. I'm sorry, Mr. Pinfold."

"Well, keep quiet then."

"That's just what I was going to suggest. Look here Gil — Mr. Pinfold, sir — let's do a deal. I'll switch off the apparatus. I promise on my honour we'll none of us ever worry you again. All we ask in return is that you don't say anything to anyone in England about us. It could ruin our whole work if it got talked about. Just say nothing, and you'll never hear from us again. Tell your wife you had noises in the head through taking those grey pills. Tell her anything you like but tell her it's all over. She'll believe you. She'll be delighted to hear it."

"I'll think it over," said Mr. Pinfold.

He thought it over. There were strong attractions

221

in the bargain. Could Angel be trusted? He was in a panic now at the prospect of getting into trouble with the B.B.C.

"Not the B.B.C., darling," said Margaret. "It isn't them that worry him. They know all about his experiments. It's Reggie Graves-Upton. *He* must never know. He's sort of cousin, you see, and he would tell our aunt and father and mother and everyone. It would cause the most frightful complications. Gilbert, you must never tell *anyone*, promise, especially not Cousin Reggie."

"And you, Meg," said Mr. Pinfold in bantering but fond tones, "are you going to leave me alone too?"

"Oh, Gilbert dearest, it's not a thing to joke about. I've so loved being with you. I shall miss you more than anyone I've ever known in my life. I shall never forget you. If my brother switches off it will be a kind of death for me. But I know I have to suffer. I'll be brave. You *must* accept the offer, Gilbert."

"I'll let you know before I reach London," said Mr. Pinfold.

Presently they were over England.

"Well," said Angel, "what's your answer?"

"I said 'London.'"

Later they were over the London airport. "Fasten your belts, please. No smoking."

"Here we are," said Angel. "Speak up. Is it a deal?"

"I don't call this London," said Mr. Pinfold.

He had cabled to his wife from Rome that he would go straight to the hotel they always used. He did not wait for the other passengers to board the bus. Instead he hired a car. Not until they were in the borough of Acton did he reply to Angel. Then he said:

"The answer is: No."

"You can't mean it." Angel was unaffectedly aghast. "Why, Mr. Pinfold, sir? Why?"

"First, because I don't accept your word of honour. You don't know what honour is. Secondly, I thoroughly dislike you and your revolting wife. You have been extremely offensive to me and I intend to make you suffer for it. Thirdly, I think your plans, your work as you call it, highly dangerous. You've driven one man to suicide, perhaps others, too, that I don't know about. You tried to drive me. Heaven knows what you've done to Roger Stillingfleet. Heaven knows who you may attack next. Apart from any private resentment I feel, I regard you as a public menace that has got to be silenced."

"All right, Gilbert, if that's the way you want it — "

"Don't call me 'Gilbert' and don't talk like a film gangster."

"All right, Gilbert. You'll pay for this."

But there was no confidence to his threats. Angel was a beaten man and knew it.

"Mrs. Pinfold arrived an hour ago," the concierge told him. "She is waiting for you in your room.'"

Mr. Pinfold took the lift, walked down the corridor and opened the door, with Goneril and Angel raucous on either side. He was shy of his wife, when they met.

"You *look* all right," she said.

"I *am* all right. I have this trouble I wrote to you about, but I hope I can get it cleared up. I'm sorry not to be more affectionate, but it's a little embarrassing having three people listening to everything one says."

"Yes," said Mrs. Pinfold. "It must be. I can see that. Have you had luncheon?"

"Hours ago, in Paris. Of course there's the difference of an hour."

"I've had none. I'll order something now."

"How you hate her, Gilbert! How she bores you!" said Goneril.

"Don't believe a word she says," said Angel.

"She's very pretty," Margaret conceded, "and very kind. But she is not good enough for you. I suppose you think I'm jealous. Well, I am."

"I'm sorry to be so uncommunicative," said Mr. Pinfold. "You see, these abominable people keep talking to me."

"Most distracting," said Mrs. Pinfold.

"Most."

The waiter brought a tray. When he had gone Mrs. Pinfold said: "You know you've got it all wrong about this Mr. Angel. As soon as I got your letter I telephoned to Arthur at the B.B.C. and inquired. Angel has been in England all the time."

"Don't listen to her. She's lying."

Mr. Pinfold was dumbfounded.

"Are you absolutely sure?"

"Ask them yourself."

Mr. Pinfold went to the telephone. He had a friend named Arthur high in the talks department.

"Arthur, that fellow who came down to interview me last summer, Angel — haven't you sent him to Aden . . . you haven't? He's in England now? . . .

No, I don't want to speak to him. . . . It's just that I ran across someone rather like him on board ship. . . . Good-bye . . . Well," he said to his wife, "I simply don't know what to make of this."

"I may as well tell you the truth," said Angel. "We never were in that ship. We worked the whole thing from the studio in England."

"They must be working the whole thing from a studio in England," said Mr. Pinfold.

"My poor darling," said Mrs. Pinfold, "no one's 'worked' anything. You're imagining it all. Just to make sure I asked Father Westmacott as you suggested. He says the whole thing's utterly impossible. There just isn't any sort of invention by the Gestapo or the B.B.C. or the Existentialists or the psycho-analysts — nothing at all, the least like what you think."

"No Box?"

"No Box."

"Don't believe her. She's lying. She's lying," said Goneril, but with every word her voice dwindled as though a great distance was being put between them. Her last word was little more than the thin grating of a slate-pencil.

"You mean that everything I've heard said, I've

been saying to myself? It's hardly conceivable."

"It's perfectly true, darling," said Margaret. "I never had a brother or a sister-in-law, no father, no mother, nothing. . . . I don't exist, Gilbert. There isn't any me, anywhere at all. . . . but I do love you, Gilbert. I don't exist but I do love . . . Good-bye . . . Love . . . " and her voice too trailed away, sank to a whisper, a sigh, the rustle of a pillow, then was silent.

Mr. Pinfold sat in the silence. There had been other occasions of seeming release which had proved illusory. This he knew was the final truth. He was alone with his wife.

"They've gone," he said at length. "In that minute. Gone for good."

"I hope that's true. What are we going to do now? I couldn't make any plans till I knew what sort of a state I'd find you in. Father Westmacott gave me the name of a man he says we can trust."

"A looney doctor?"

"A psychologist — but a Catholic so he must be all right."

"No," said Mr. Pinfold. "I've had enough of psychology. How about taking the tea train home?"

Mrs. Pinfold hesitated. She had come to London

prepared to see her husband into a nursing-home. She said: "Are you sure you oughtn't to see somebody?"

"I might see Drake," said Mr. Pinfold.

So they went to Paddington and took their seats in the restaurant car. It was full of neighbours returning from a day's shopping. They ate toasted buns and the familiar landscape rolled past invisible in the dark and misted window panes.

"We heard you'd gone to the tropics, Gilbert."

"Just back."

"You didn't stay long. Was it boring?"

"No," said Mr. Pinfold, "not the least boring. It was most exciting. But I had enough."

Their neighbours always had thought Mr. Pinfold rather odd.

"But it *was* exciting," said Mr. Pinfold when he and his wife were alone in the car driving home. "It was the most exciting thing, really, that ever happened to me," and during the days which followed he recounted every detail of his long ordeal.

The hard frost had given place to fog and intermittent sleet. The house was as cold as ever but Mr. Pinfold was content to sit over the fire and, like a warrior returned from a hard-fought victory, relive his trials, endurances and achievements. No sound troubled him from that other half-world into which he had stumbled, but there was nothing dreamlike about his experiences. They remained undiminished and unobscured, as sharp and hard as any event of his waking life. "What I can't understand is this," he said. "If I was supplying all the information to the Angels, why did I tell them such a lot of rot? I mean to say, if I wanted to draw up an indictment of myself, I could make a far blacker and more plausible case than they did. I can't understand."

Mr. Pinfold never has understood this; nor has anyone been able to suggest a plausible explanation.

"You know," he said, some evenings later, "I was very near accepting Angel's offer. Supposing I had, and the voices had stopped just as they have done now, I should have believed that that infernal Box existed. All my life I should have lived in the fear that at any moment the whole thing might start up again. Or for all I knew they might just have been listening all the time and not saying anything. It would have been an awful situation."

"It was very brave of you to turn down the offer," said Mrs. Pinfold.

"It was sheer bad temper," said Mr. Pinfold quite truthfully.

"All the same, I think you ought to see a doctor. There must have been something the matter with you."

"Just those pills," said Mr. Pinfold.

They were his last illusion. When finally Dr. Drake came Mr. Pinfold said: "Those grey pills you gave me. They were pretty strong."

"They seem to have worked," said Dr. Drake.

"Could that have made me hear voices?"

"Good heavens no."

"Not if they were mixed with bromide and chloral?"

"There wasn't any chloral in the mixture I gave you."

"No. But to tell you the truth I had a bottle of my own."

Dr. Drake did not seem shocked by the revelation. "That is always a trouble with private patients," he said. "One never knows what else they're taking on the quiet. I've known people make themselves thoroughly ill."

"I was thoroughly ill. I heard voices for nearly a fortnight."

230

"And they've stopped now?"

"Yes."

"And you've stopped the bromide and chloral?"

"Yes."

"Then I don't think we have far to look. I should keep off that mixture if I were you. It can't be the right thing for you. I'll send something else. Those voices were pretty offensive, I suppose?"

"Abominably. How did you know?"

"They always are. Lots of people hear voices from time to time — nearly always offensive."

"You don't think he ought to see a psychologist?" asked Mrs. Pinfold.

"He can if he likes, of course, but it sounds like a perfectly simple case of poisoning to me."

"That's a relief," said Mrs. Pinfold, but Mr. Pinfold accepted this diagnosis less eagerly. He knew, and the others did not know — not even his wife, least of all his medical adviser — that he had endured a great ordeal and, unaided, had emerged the victor. There was a triumph to be celebrated, even if a mocking slave stood always beside him in his chariot reminding him of mortality.

Next day was Sunday. After Mass Mr. Pinfold said:

"You know I can't face the Bruiser. It's going to

231

be several weeks before I can talk to him about his Box. Have a fire lighted in the library. I'm going to do some writing."

As the wood crackled and a barely perceptible warmth began to spread among the chilly shelves, Mr. Pinfold sat down to work for the first time since his fiftieth birthday. He took the pile of manuscript, his unfinished novel, from the drawer and glanced through it. The story was still clear in his mind. He knew what had to be done. But there was more urgent business first, a hamper to be unpacked of fresh, rich experience — perishable goods.

He returned the manuscript to the drawer, spread a new quire of foolscap before him and wrote in his neat, steady hand:

The Ordeal of Gilbert Pinfold
A Conversation Piece
Chapter One
Portrait of the Artist in Middle Age